The Case of Secrets

ALL CLASSIC
—— BOOKS ——

ISBN-10: 1-938759-11-7
ISBN-13: 978-1-938759-11-6

The Case of Secrets is available in trade paperback. For bulk discount orders or other questions, contact us at info@allclassicbooks.com.

All Classic Books
Manufactured in the United States of America

The Case of Secrets

Alfred M. Struthers

Dedication

For Kristen and Ryan

Prologue

October 20, 1903

It was a brutal night. The howling wind swept past the front window of the bookshop, carrying with it a torrent of leaves, small branches and debris. The horse-drawn carriages that rumbled by the front door throughout the day were silent now—safely put away for the stormy night that promised trouble for any traveler who dared to challenge it.

The main floor of the shop was still and quiet. Working alone in the back room, the bookstore owner busied himself emptying wooden boxes packed with books. He meticulously sorted them into piles, which had grown so large that they now covered the entire table.

The last of his customers had left hours ago, yet he continued to work despite the wind that rattled the front door, begging to be let in. He paid the muffled noises from outside no mind, as he pushed up his glasses and devoured each title, lost in the world of covers and spines and pages.

This latest batch of books had come from an estate sale in the neighboring town of Concord, Massachusetts. Luckily, the merchants and scavengers who attended the sale were much too interested in the oriental rugs and heirloom jewelry to bother with a wagonload of outdated books. To their untrained eyes, old books were nothing more than ancient relics. But the shopkeeper knew otherwise, as he should; he'd been well trained like those who came before him.

At the sale his pulse quickened when he first discovered the vast collection carelessly tossed into boxes and pushed into a dark corner of the study. Without delay, he located the seller and finalized the sale with a handful of crisp bills.

"And there's more, if you have them loaded in my wagon immediately."

Now, as he worked his way through each box, by the soft light of his candle lantern, he took great care with every volume, scanning page after page. When a certain word or phrase caught his eye, he'd stop and examine it further. Other times, all it took was a photo. After inspections, the books were placed on one of two piles.

The first was a mountainous stack, arranged by author and subject matter. In the morning it would be moved to the main floor of the shop, and in the coming days would be picked over carefully by the shop's dedicated regulars.

The second pile would stay behind. It would be much smaller—three, maybe four books if he was lucky—but much more important nonetheless. They would never see the front window, the sale counter, or any of the shelves that lined the perimeter of the shop. Instead, they would reside in a special place—an old bookcase tucked away in the furthest corner of the back room. Out of sight. Away from curious eyes.

Where the bookcase originated was a mystery. But it had come a long way, that much was evident. On its dark wooden shelves was an assortment of books like no other, collected over countless years and for one simple reason: each contained a secret that had been buried and forgotten. Lost over time.

With it came an obligation that the shopkeeper knew all too well. It was his birthright, and for his remaining years he would work to unravel the veiled secret in each book. When the opportunity presented itself, as it had on this day, he would add to the collection. For there were more books just like these.

Books with secrets.

And another family member to follow.

Chapter One

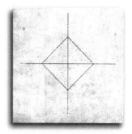

Compton's Journal

He hated it here. Not just because of the darkness, or the smell, or the broken floorboards. It was the spiders. They were everywhere—waiting for you the minute you walked into the room. They'd crawl on you...bite you...make you wish you never walked through the door in the first place. That's the way Nathan Cole was feeling at the moment—the way he felt *every* time his parents made him come to the attic. Things would be very different if it were up to him. Not that much was up to an 11-year-old.

At the attic door he paused and took a deep breath. The plan was simple—go in, drop off the box, leave...the quicker the better. Gathering his nerve, he exhaled, took hold of the doorknob and gave it a turn. The painful squeal it emitted was a warning...*this is your last chance*...but he ignored it and pushed through the door. Little did he know what surprise awaited him on the other side.

The light switch was on the wall to his left, and as his fingers fumbled in the darkness trying to find it, something landed in his hair. After several frantic swipes at it, when he was certain it was gone, or dead, he flicked the light switch and then turned around.

"You've got to be kidding me."

It was even worse than the last time. There was more and more of everything, piled higher and deeper, choking off what little space remained. A narrow pathway meandered through the middle of the room and disappeared around the corner just past the chimney. But the chimney was as far as he'd go, ever since the spiders claimed the small window nearby and covered it with webs, smothering what little light it once offered.

With a heavy sigh he quickly moved forward, squeezing past the ancient relics that time forgot. He was still fuming about giving up a perfectly good Saturday to help his parents clean the basement. And for what? So his Dad could set up an office? His elbow clipped an old coat stand, knocking it onto a stack of plastic tubs, and he yelled, "Could we cram any *more* junk in here?"

It didn't help that he was carrying a box of old dishes that no one would ever use. If it were up to him, they'd get thrown in the trash.

One at a time.

But no, his mother insisted they be saved. And where else? In the attic of course.

Halfway across the room he had to turn his body to avoid a pair of overstuffed garment bags that were hanging from a rafter. They were caked with dust and a thick tangle of spider webs connected them. "Unbelievable," he whispered as he moved deeper into the shadows.

I could be outside right now…

The floorboards creaked under his feet.

Riding my bike.
They sounded angry.
Instead of here…
He reached the chimney and paused.
In this dump.
There was an opening along the wall, next to the window, between a rocking chair and an old steamer trunk, so he hurried over and set the box on the floor. "So long," he said as he pushed it against the wall with his foot, "I hope you like spiders."

He turned around to leave when the deathly quiet of the room was shattered by a loud thud. It was so sudden that he fell backwards onto the trunk and bumped his head on the wall, knocking down an old picture frame in the process.

"WHO'S THERE?" he shouted. There was no answer. He climbed to his feet, rubbing his aching head. That's when he discovered the source of the noise; it was an old book, lying in the middle of the walkway, several feet away. "ALL RIGHT, VERY FUNNY," he called out as he stumbled over and picked it up.

He peered through the broken light and shadows, towards the door, to see who snuck in the room when he wasn't looking.

Trying to scare me.
But there was no one else in the room, and a nervous twinge rippled through his body.
If there's no one else here...
He looked down at the book in his hand.
Then where did this come from?
He looked up slowly, his eyes sweeping cautiously around the room. *Wait...*

Several feet away, tucked back in the shadows, he spied a bookcase. It looked ancient, packed with old books, just like the one in his hand, and there was an empty slot on one of the shelves.

"Impossible."

He looked at the book and then back at the empty slot.

"How did you get from there to...?"

Out of the corner of his eye, he saw something move. It was a small brown blur, dangling just inches from his face. In a panic he jumped aside before it could land on him, and he tumbled headlong over a short stack of cardboard boxes. They crumpled under his weight as he crashed to the floor.

"OWW!" he moaned, rubbing his elbow. He pushed himself up off the filth-covered floor, still clutching the book, and found himself directly in front of the bookcase. What he saw there made him forget about spiders.

He was tall for his age, over five feet, but the bookcase towered over him. It was well over six feet high and sat up off the floor on thick bun feet. There were four shelves on the top and four more on the bottom, flanked on each side by thick Doric columns. Running across the middle was a row of small drawers, no more than three inches high. They were each decorated with an elaborate half-moon pull forged from solid brass, that had dulled with age.

He had no idea where the bookcase came from, and he couldn't remember seeing it during his previous trips to the attic. Not that he'd pay much attention to an old bookcase anyway. The books that lined its shelves were too old and too boring to be of any interest to him. The thought of having to read them made him shudder. It was bad enough that he had to read every night for school. That was painful.

He pushed the thought away and quickly slid the book into the empty slot, then made a mad dash towards the door.

I'm outta here...

He almost made it.

Another loud thud broke the silence of the room, and when he looked back over his shoulder he tripped on a floorboard and fell to the floor. "What now?" he griped as he stood up and turned around. The book was lying on the floor again—in the exact same place. "What the...?" he whispered, as he stood there scanning the room from corner to corner. His heart was pounding. "WHO DID THAT?" Again, there was no answer, and he quickly went back and picked it up for a second time. With shaking hands he hurried over to the bookcase and shoved it on the shelf, this time using both hands. That's when something very strange happened.

The book pushed back.

"HEY." He yanked his hands away as if he'd touched a hot iron. After a moment's hesitation, he reached out very slowly and nudged the book gently into the slot. But before he could pull his hand away, it slid right back out. "No way," he exclaimed, his eyes wide. Then he got an idea. He took a deep breath and exhaled loudly. "Let's see you stop *this*." Using every bit of strength he had, he gave the book a hard shove into the opening and this time it stayed put. "That's more like it," he said triumphantly.

The words were barely out of his mouth when the book exploded off the shelf and hit him square in the stomach. It was so abrupt that it knocked all 90 pounds of him backwards onto an old coffee table, and with one lightning quick motion he snatched the book out of the air as he toppled onto the floor.

"All right, I've had it," he said, as he jumped to his feet. He pushed the loose hair out of his face and then brushed himself off, just in case any stray spiders had climbed aboard. When he was sure he was spider-free, he looked at the book, then back at the bookcase. "It's a bookcase...an old bookcase...nothing more."

He bit his lower lip and moved closer, leaning in to get a better look at the opening on the shelf. In the dark of the room, it was impossible to see anything. He took another deep breath and reached into the opening with his fingers, feeling along the smooth finish of the wood. "Books don't just fall off shelves," he stated with authority.

And they don't fly off shelves, either.

He slid his fingers all the way to the back of the bookcase, but the slot was empty—there was nothing but the silken finish of aged wood, worn smooth over a lifetime by countless books. That left only one other possibility, and it brought a devious smile to his face. It was some kind of trick book—a completely normal-looking book that doesn't stay on the shelf.

"THAT'S AWESOME!"

He laughed out loud, thinking about the fun he would have with it at school. Especially in the library. He turned it over in his hands, giving each side a close inspection. Whoever made it was a genius, he thought, because it looked totally authentic. The binding, the front and back covers, even the edges of the pages had been constructed to look just like an ordinary book. There was nothing on the outside to give it away. Then he opened the front cover.

He had opened plenty of books in his life, usually against his will. Dozens, hundreds, who knows how many? Paperbacks, hard covers, it made no difference. Books were all the same—tiresome. Except for comic books...those were OK. But every other kind of book usually led to something bad...like homework...endless annoying homework. Books also meant sitting in class studying things like, triangles with funny names and complex equations. Things he'd never use in his entire lifetime. What he didn't know, as he stood in the dim light of the attic, was that *this* book was not like any of the others.

The binding creaked like an old wicker chair. Then came another sound. At first it was like a gentle wisp of wind, the kind that rustles the leaves in the large oak tree behind the house. But then it changed pitch, and he knew it wasn't the kind of sound the wind makes—it was the kind of sound a human makes—the slow and steady exhale after a long restful nap, when you sit up and wipe the sleep from your eyes.

The moment he heard it, he slammed the book shut, and with his whole body shaking he spun around to see if someone was hiding behind him in the shadows.

"Who's there," he tried to shout. It came out no louder than a whisper.

It was time to drop it and run. But then he heard it—the voice. It whispered to him from some far off place in the back of his mind, in a tone that was reckless and unafraid.

Books don't breathe.

It reverberated through his whole body.

People breathe, animals breathe…

He couldn't turn it off or push it away.

You imagined it.

Then it began to reason.

It's just an old book.

Began to push.

What could be more harmless than that?

17

And then it dared him.

You want to be sure...don't you?

He took a deep breath and then slowly opened the book, fully expecting to hear the strange breathing sound again. But this time there was nothing. He let out a long breath of his own and felt the nervousness slowly leaving his body. His heart rate slowed back down to normal as he laughed at his own silliness.

I just imagined it.

He couldn't believe he'd been so afraid.

It's nothing...

Or so gullible.

Just an old book...

To prove it, he took a closer look at the first page. The paper was old and thin, but the print was still clear enough to read.

Compton's Journal Of Architectural Marvels
Design Masters of the 19th Century

Compiled by Owen W. Compton, III

"Delightful," he mumbled in a disgusted voice as he flipped the page to the Table of Contents. It was even worse—nothing but a long list of chapters, each one dedicated to some builder or architect from the past century. There was Austin and Burnham, Blackall and Brimmer; someone named Bryant and another by the name of Bulfinch. That one actually sounded funny.

The list went on and on with names like Cummings, Davis, McIntyre and Parris. He was just about to close the book when something extraordinary happened. If he hadn't seen it with his own eyes, he'd never believe such a thing could happen.

The page turned all by itself.

It was like an invisible hand reached over his shoulder and turned it before he could do it himself.

He slammed the book shut and held it out at arm's length. "I didn't imagine THAT!" His arm trembled as he stood there holding it as far from his body as possible.

"NATHAN?"

His father was calling from the second floor.

"YEAH?" he shouted towards the door.

He heard his father's heavy footsteps climbing the attic stairs.

HE'S COMING UP!

In a panic, he looked for a place to stash the book. The bookcase was definitely out. Every cardboard box he saw was taped shut. Then he spied an old bureau with four large drawers over in the corner.

Perfect.

He started to wind his way over to it when he heard a loud thump on the attic door.

"NATHAN, GET THE DOOR FOR ME."

He shook both of his arms in frustration.

"HOLD ON," he yelled.

He turned and made a mad dash through the clutter, knocking into boxes and bags along the way. When he reached the door, slightly out of breath, he pulled it open and saw his dad standing there holding a large box of dishes with both hands.

19

"Your mother found these right after you left."

Nathan stood there with a nervous knot in his stomach, holding the book in his left hand, hidden behind the door.

"Well...are you going to let me in?" his father asked impatiently.

"Oh...yeah...sorry." He stepped back and pulled the door open all the way.

His father walked into the room and stopped short. "Wow!"

Nathan rolled his eyes. "Yeah, tell me about it." Then he got an idea. He pointed across the room with his free hand. "There's a good spot over there...on the far wall...that's where I put the other dishes."

His father squinted as he looked across the room, craning his neck to see where Nathan was pointing. "Really? Looks pretty jammed to me. How about you show me?"

Nathan gulped. "Uh...sure Dad."

So much for that idea.

He transferred the book behind his back, from his left hand to his right hand, in one smooth move, and then stepped away from the door. If he kept the book tight against the side of his body his father wouldn't notice it and maybe he could...

OWW!

His right foot hit something on the floor, and he nearly tripped. When he looked down, he saw an old wicker laundry basket with thick woven handles.

Bingo!

Very casually he lowered his hand down and dropped the book into the basket, and then pushed it back into the shadows with his foot. Problem solved.

"Follow me, Dad."

They squeezed along the narrow pathway, ducking spider webs and trying not to knock anything over. When they reached the far wall, his dad set the box of dishes down and let out a heavy sigh. "This place is unbelievable."

"That's what I said," Nathan muttered, swatting at something dangling in front of his face. "Can we go now?"

His father was brushing spider webs from the top of his head. "Yeah, I've had about enough."

They worked their way back through the clutter. Just as they got to the door his father said, "Hold on, I just remembered, your mother asked me to bring something back with me."

"Bring something back...from here?" *Are you nuts?*

"Yeah...baby clothes. She said they were right here near the door."

Nathan froze.

Near the door?

The basket was near the door. He never got a good look at what was in it, but just to be safe, he inched over and stood in front of it, hiding it from view.

His father checked the jumble of bags and boxes to the right of the door. "She said they were right here somewhere...in some plastic bags."

Nathan looked left and right. "No plastic bags over here, Dad."

"Well," his father sighed, "they're not over here either."

Nathan let out a nervous breath.

"I guess she'll just have to come up here and...wait a minute...I think they're right there." He was looking at the floor next to Nathan's feet.

Nathan glanced down to his left, then his right. "Nope...not here."

21

"Sure...right there...behind you."

Nathan shot a quick glance over his shoulder. "Sorry."

"No, down *there*." He pointed at Nathan's feet.

Nathan turned around and pretended to look. "Really Dad, I don't see..."

"In the *basket*," his father said. "Your mother said they were in an old laundry basket."

He reached down and pulled the basket out from the shadows. It was packed with clear plastic bags, each jammed with his old baby clothes.

"Oh...*this* basket."

"That's the one. You carry it downstairs, I'll get the light."

"Are you sure Dad? I mean, this basket is pretty ratty...and these baby clothes are really old. They probably smell."

"I'm sure. Now let's go. We've got lots to do downstairs."

Nathan sighed. "Whatever." He leaned over reluctantly and, with one hand, he grabbed one of the handles. With his other hand he shoved the book deep into the basket between the plastic bags. This was going from bad to worse. All he wanted to do was hide the book, but now it was going downstairs where his mother was going to find it and start asking questions. Unless...

I'll put the basket in my room.

He picked it up and carried it out the door.

Until later.

And down the creaky attic stairs.

Then I'll take the book back upstairs to the attic and forget about it altogether.

He reached the bottom of the stairs and walked quickly down the hallway towards his bedroom.

"Wait," his father said, as he closed the door to the third floor. "Leave the basket here in the hallway. Knowing your mom, she'll want to sort through them."

Nathan stopped quick.

No...not the hallway.

"Uh...it's OK Dad," he said, like it was no big deal, "I can put it in my room for now."

His father walked down the hallway. "No, right here is fine."

"Right here? In the hallway? What if somebody..."

His father took the basket out of his hands. "What is it with you and this basket?" He set it down on the floor. "Now come on, time's a wastin'." He took a few steps down the hallway and then stopped. Nathan still hadn't budged from the basket. "Nathan? LET'S GO."

"All right, all right." He walked tentatively away from the basket like an invisible force field was holding him back. As he followed his father downstairs, his anxiety grew with each step and he knew he'd have to sneak back upstairs and get the book before his mother found it.

If he didn't, bad things would follow.

"Ah...there are my brave soldiers," his mom declared, as they came down the basement stairs. She was busy piling old magazines into a recycling tub. "Did you find a good home for the dishes?"

"You could say that," his father quipped. "I think they should be safe for the next hundred years or so."

Nathan nodded in agreement and then went back to the boring chore he was given before his trek up to the attic—loading old puzzles into a storage tub.

"Did you find the basket of baby clothes?" his mother asked.

"We did," his father answered. "It's upstairs in the hallway."

His mother flashed a thumbs up. "Perfect. I'll run up later and go through them. I'm sure Nathan doesn't mind if we give them away...right Nathan?"

Nathan froze, and his eyes went wide at the thought of his mother reaching into the basket and finding the book...the questions that would follow...her reaction when she turned back the cover and saw the pages start to...

"Nathan? What's wrong?" she asked, her eyebrows knit with concern.

"Huh?" He dropped the puzzle box he was holding and it landed on its side, spilling puzzle pieces onto the floor.

"Are you all right?" She put down the magazine she was holding.

"Um...yeah...." He quickly knelt down and began scooping up puzzle pieces as the bizarre events in the attic pinballed through his mind.

A book that flies?

Impossible.

Pages that flip by themselves?

Never.

Breathing sounds?

That just doesn't happen.

But it DID happen—he saw it with his own eyes. He was still struggling to make sense of it all when he heard his name. It was faint, like someone calling to him from outside the house.

"Nathan?"

He snapped out of his funk and looked up. His mother was standing there, staring down at him, her eyes studying him curiously, as if he were a rare tropical bird. It was the

24

same face she made when he tried to explain his math homework.

"Yeah?" He had no idea she'd been standing there for a full minute, watching him.

"Are you OK?"

"Me? I'm fine. Just thinking, that's all." He closed the puzzle box and climbed to his feet.

"What about?" she asked.

He didn't have an answer. What could he say?

I just found this crazy book up in the attic and wait 'till you hear what it did?

Never.

Not in a million years.

She stood there staring at him, waiting for an answer. Thinking quickly, he tried another approach.

"Um..." he began, shoving the puzzle into the plastic tub. "You know that old bookcase up in the attic?"

"Yes. What about it?"

"Where did it come from?"

She smiled. "That was your grandfather's. It used to be in his bookstore."

A fuzzy image emerged in Nathan's memory.

"Do you remember? We took you there many times. He had lots of old, rare books."

"Yeah...a little bit," he said slowly, as the image lingered in his mind.

"Well...let me think." She scratched the side of her head. "You're 11 years old now, so you were almost 6 years old when he died. It's feels like forever ago but it really wasn't, not when you think about it. Anyway, after your grandfather died, we sold the store. His bookcase was the only thing we kept."

Nathan's face was twisted with confusion. "Why?"

She shrugged. "He was very fond of it. Probably because it belonged to *his* father, who was your great grandfather."

"What about the books in it...the bookcase, I mean?"

"What about them?"

"Why did he save them? I mean, if he had a store, why didn't he sell them?"

"I'm not sure." She bent down to tie off a plastic trash bag that was bulging to capacity. "I imagine they were special editions. Your grandfather was quite the book collector." Then she looked over at him. "Why the sudden interest in that old bookcase?"

"Uh...just curious."

She started to pick up the trash bag when he got an idea. "No, don't do that Mom, I'll get it." He grabbed the bag and dragged it out the side door and around to the garage, all the while thinking about something his mother said.

Special editions?

What did that mean exactly? Special in what way?

Like the book upstairs in the hallway?

The thought gave him the chills, and he shook it off as he flung the trash bag into the corner of the garage. Then he raced across the lawn to the back door of the house.

If I hurry...

He slipped into the back hall.

I can sneak upstairs...

Up the short stairway into the kitchen.

And get back down to the basement...

Then into the center hallway.

Before they get suspicious.

He hurried down the hallway, fighting the urge to run. He was just starting up the front stairs when he heard his mother's voice. "Oh there you are." His foot stopped in midair, and he looked over to see her standing in the living room. "I've got the *perfect* job for you."

He turned slowly and trudged down the steps.

There ARE no perfect jobs.

"Take this down to the office," she said, handing him a box marked 'FILES,' "and then come right back. There are plenty more where that came from."

He closed his eyes and let out a heavy breath.

You have GOT to be kidding me.

Twenty minutes later, when he finished hauling boxes, he hurried up the basement stairs for another try. He got as far as the top step when his father appeared in the doorway holding a rolled up rug. "Look at that...perfect timing. You can put this against the wall. I'll unroll it later."

Nathan sighed and flopped his head to one side.

This is never going to end.

He took hold of the rug and wrestled it down the stairs, trying to keep it from unrolling. When he finally got it over to the wall, he was just about to drop it when he heard his mother say, "Oh not *that* rug." She was standing across the room, dusting the shade on a tall desk lamp. "I have another one for down here."

He shook his head in disbelief. "You know, I wish you guys would..." he started to groan.

"Oh come on," she coaxed, walking towards him. "I'll help you take it upstairs."

Upstairs? His pulse quickened. "Yes...we should...I mean...definitely...that's a good idea."

They each grabbed an end and muscled the rug up the basement stairs. As they carried it up the front hall stairway, Nathan's heart was pounding.

Can't let her look in the basket...

When they reached the top landing and started down the hallway, his hands were shaking so much he nearly dropped the rug.

"Oh, look at that," his mother said in a sentimental voice, as she paused next to the basket, "your old baby clothes."

"Yeah Mom, I *know*..." he grumbled. "Can we keep going please? This is heavy."

"All right," she said in her best Nathan imitation. They continued up the hallway and stopped when they reached the guest room door. "Let's set it here against the wall. I have to move some boxes before we take it in. It'll just take a second."

They plunked the rug down on the floor, and his mother disappeared into the guest room.

Nathan's heart raced.

This is my chance.

He heard the sound of boxes sliding across the wooden floor and his mother mumbling to herself.

GO! NOW!

He raced back to the laundry basket, figuring he had 30 seconds, maybe less, before his mother reappeared in the hallway. That was more than enough time for him to run the book to his room, toss it inside and close the door.

With both hands he rummaged through the basket, shoving the plastic bags aside in a wild frenzy. His panic surged when he pulled back the last bag and saw the overlapping strands of wicker at the bottom of the basket.

The book was gone.

Chapter Two

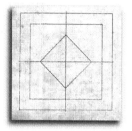

Gina

He stared blankly into the basket, too stunned to move. Then, one by one, each of his senses awoke as if the world was being revealed to him for the very first time. He felt the smooth give of the plastic bags against his fingertips and smelled the stale odor of the attic that clung to them like an invisible layer of skin. His eyes followed the subtle weave of thick rattan at the bottom of the basket.

The faint creak of a floorboard registered in his ears and he spun around to see his mother standing in the hallway. "What are you doing?" she asked in a bewildered voice.

He turned back to the basket and began hastily straightening the plastic bags. "Nothing."

"Were you *looking* for something?"

He let out a nervous laugh. "Me? Looking for something?" He couldn't meet her eyes. "No," he said defensively. "I just saw these crazy baby clothes."

She cocked her head slightly, looking at him, the basket, then back at him again. He didn't look up to see her piercing stare or wrinkled eyebrows, that gave away her feelings of suspicion. .

"I mean...just look at them," he said, quickly turning one of the bags over in his hand. "They're tiny."

"Yes Nathan, I know that, I bought them for you, remember?" She turned to the rolled up rug at her feet and let out a heavy breath. "Well...come on...we'd better get this rug into the guest room. Dinner's going to be late enough as it is."

Nathan slowly climbed to his feet, holding on to the basket for support and to steady his trembling hands.

This makes no sense.

They hoisted the rug and snaked it into the guest room. Once it was in place, Nathan went back out to the hallway and eyed the basket suspiciously.

Books don't just disappear.

A hand touched his shoulder. "Everything OK?"

He flinched. "Huh? Oh...yeah."

"Good," she said, putting her arm around him. "Then you can come downstairs and help me peel potatoes." She playfully tousled his hair and then went down to the kitchen. Normally, he would put up a fight, but he was too preoccupied with the troubling question that burned in his mind.

Where did the book go?

The main topic of discussion at the dinner table was a new printer for the office, and as Nathan's parents bantered on and on, he quickly tuned them out. The riddle of the book's whereabouts tormented him like a word problem in math class—the kind that drove him crazy. It usually started with something like, "If Janie picked 3 bushels of apples and Tommy picked 2 bushels..."

His version was more frustrating.

I hid the book in the basket...

He reached for the mashed potatoes.

I brought the basket downstairs...

And spooned a large dollop onto his plate.

Went back later and it was gone...

He eyed the glazed carrots.

And no one said anything about finding it.

Then it came to him.

What's the problem here?

All he wanted to do was leave the book in the attic where no one would see it. Now it had mysteriously vanished.

Isn't that the same thing?

He had no idea how it happened, but the book was gone—his problem was solved. It was time to forget about it and move on.

His parents were still talking about printers, so he gobbled down the rest of his dinner and snuck up to his bedroom before he got roped into washing the dishes. The laundry basket was still sitting in the hallway. He gave it a fleeting glance and snickered just before he ducked into his bedroom and closed the door.

Not my problem anymore.

He was halfway across the room when something caught his eye and he stumbled on the rug, nearly falling over.

Wait a minute.

The book was sitting on his desk.

Where did that come from?

A cold chill slowly crept up his back, and he nibbled on the inside of his lip.

That can't be the same book...

He gulped and then slowly walked over to the desk. When he picked up the book and turned back the front cover to the title page, what he saw sent a nervous jolt through his entire body.

Compton's Journal of Architectural Marvels.

He had barely finished reading when the pages started turning, all by themselves, and he flung the book down on the desk. "STOP IT," he shouted, backing away. But the pages continued to turn…two, three, four at a time. Then, as suddenly as they started, they stopped.

The room was perfectly still, except for the sound of Nathan's rapidly beating heart and quick breaths. A few seconds passed, and then he took a small step forward. Then another. When he was close enough to touch it, he reached out with one lightning-quick motion and closed the book. But just as he started to breathe a sigh of relief, it flew open again. This time it startled him so much that he stumbled backwards and tripped on the rug, landing on the floor with a dull thud.

"It's just a book…it's just a book…" he kept telling himself as he got to his feet.

The book sat perfectly still on his desk, and for several moments he just stood there staring at it, trying to decide what to do next. Finally, he moved towards it again. This time he didn't try to close it; he poked it with his finger, moving it a few inches across the top of the desk. Nothing happened. He nudged it again, a little harder. It slid a few more inches and stopped…then nothing. That's when he decided it was safe to take a closer look.

He leaned over the desk, holding his hair out of his face with one hand while he looked down at the open pages. The first thing he noticed was a man's face looking back up at him. It was an old picture, faded and scratchy, and right below it, printed in bold type, was a name.

Alastair Raven.

Raven?

That was a cool name.

He read the first few sentences on the page. Then a few more. Before long he was well into the second paragraph and without realizing it, he did the unthinkable—he picked up the book and took it over to his bed, never once taking his eyes from the page.

As he lay in bed reading, strange words and complex images flooded his mind. Finally, he couldn't keep his eyes open for another second. He never felt the book slip out of his hands and fall to his side.

Sleep had already taken him.

The next morning when he woke, Nathan climbed out of bed, sleepy-eyed and hungry. His hair was the usual tangle atop his head, making it look like he'd combed it with a brick. He squinted as he stumbled across the room and went downstairs to breakfast. Soon after he began his second bowl of cereal, he remembered the book and the events of the previous day, and his mind was besieged with questions.

Like the first raindrops of an impending storm, they came slowly at first and then gradually picked up speed. Before long it was a downpour.

Why does a book just fall off a shelf?

How can it make breathing noises?

What makes pages turn all by themselves?

Who put it in my room?

Nathan stared off into space, thinking. None of it made any sense, and even if he wanted to there was no one he could talk to about it. Who would believe him? Who would admit that such things were even possible?

No one.

There was a simple solution—just put the book back in the attic and forget about it. Close the door and let it go. But he couldn't let it go. Not yet. Something in the book had sparked his curiosity—something to do with the man in the photo. Alastair Raven. He couldn't remember what it was, because he'd been half asleep when he read it the night before. It was drifting somewhere in the back of his mind, just out of reach. What he needed to do was read the chapter again. Now that he was fully awake, the nagging detail that was eluding him was bound to resurface.

He slurped up the last of his breakfast and threw his bowl in the sink, then ran all the way upstairs, skipping steps as he went. For the first time he was actually anxious to read a book, but when he stepped into his bedroom, things took another strange turn.

For the second time in as many days, the book was nowhere in sight.

"Not again," he groaned as he checked his bed and the surrounding area. When that turned up nothing he checked everywhere else. No box went unopened; no shelf went uninspected. He looked in each of his bureau drawers, emptied his laundry hamper and even tore through his old toy box. After that he searched the entire second floor— every room, every closet, every cabinet, shelf and drawer, even the laundry basket—but the book was nowhere to be seen. For a brief moment he thought about checking the third floor, but it was almost noontime, and he was starving.

The attic can wait.

He went downstairs and walked into the kitchen just as his dad was coming in from the garage.

"Nathan, could you give me a hand for a few minutes?"

"Right now? It's lunchtime."

"Come on, this won't take long."

He let out a long breath and followed his dad outside to the car that was parked in the driveway. The trunk was open and there was a large cardboard box wedged inside.

"I need a hand carrying this to my office," his father said.

"Whatever."

They lifted the box out of the trunk and carried it around to the corner of the house, to the side door. When they stepped into the basement, Nathan couldn't believe the difference. The room looked nothing like it had the day before. Things were arranged on the desk, the computer was set up, and there were pictures on the walls.

As he stood looking around the room, his father opened the box to reveal a brand new filing cabinet. "OK," he said to Nathan, tilting it back, "you grab that end."

Nathan sighed and took hold of the bottom of the file cabinet. "Where are we taking it?" he asked, lifting it off the ground. It was lighter that he expected.

"Right over there," his father answered, nodding to an open space on the wall. Right next to it was a small table.

Nathan took one look at the table and dropped the file cabinet on the floor. It landed with a dull metallic *clunk*.

"HEY!" his father snapped, "what are you doing?"

"My book," Nathan exclaimed. It was sitting on the table in plain sight. *How did it get down here?*

"What book?" his father asked.

"Uh...just a book...for school," Nathan stammered, picking up the bottom of the file cabinet. They carried it over to the wall and slid it into place, then Nathan quickly grabbed the book off the table and tucked it under his arm, hiding it from view.

"You sound rather surprised to see it."

"No...I just...ah.. forgot where I left it, that's all."

"I see," his dad replied. "And why would you bring one of your schoolbooks down here?"

"Uh..." he started to say. The room went totally silent as he stood dumfounded, his mind racing to come up with an answer that made sense.

"Take better care of your things," his father said, breaking the silence, "and you won't lose them. Understand?"

Nathan quickly nodded and then raced back upstairs. He had no idea how the book got downstairs to the basement, but until he could figure it out, he'd put it in a place where no one would find it.

"This should work," he said as he shoved it in the drawer of his desk. He slid it way in the back, beneath a mess of notepads, school papers and old assignment books.

Out of sight, out of mind...until after lunch.

With that problem solved, he went back downstairs to eat lunch. He was halfway through his sandwich when the telephone rang on the far wall. His mother answered it and then handed him the receiver.

"It's for you."

"Hello?" he managed to say, chewing a mouthful of food.

"It's me."

"Hey Gina, what's up?"

"Did you forget something?" she asked.

His eyes widened and he stopped chewing.

"Um...I don't know...did I?"

"You were supposed to come over, REMEMBER?"

36

"Come over...what for?"

Gina exhaled loudly.

"Our project? For school? Don't tell me you forgot about it."

"Uh..." he replied, trying to think of a good excuse. Between the basement cleaning project and his trip to the attic, that's exactly what he'd done. But now that the book had turned up again, the only thing he wanted to do was take it back to the attic before it disappeared again. Gina McDermott was not going to let that happen.

"Well?" He let out a long breath and then grumbled under his breath, "May as well get it over with."

"What was that?"

"Nothing. I'll get my stuff and be right over."

He hung up the phone and grabbed his backpack from the hall. "There goes another perfectly good afternoon."

And my chance to dump that strange book behind the first pile of boxes I find in the attic.

Gina was waiting for him at the front door. Her cinnamon hair was pulled back behind her head in a thick braid and a pencil was wedged behind her right ear. The look on her face said it all.

"You FORGOT about our project?" she cracked. She never forgot about anything. Her eyes bore into him without blinking. "We've only been working on it every day at school, or did you forget about that, too?" She was giving him her *sometimes-I-wonder-how-you-make-it-through-the-day* face.

Nathan said nothing as he pushed past her into the house.

"What, no snappy answer?" she asked, falling in behind him.

"I lost something," he said, shrugging his shoulders, "and I was busy looking for it."

Gina rolled her eyes as she followed him down the hallway.

I bet you were.

When they got to the kitchen, Nathan saw a platoon of pens and markers on the kitchen table, perfectly positioned around their project—a large poster board with a map of the United States.

"Got enough pens?"

Gina slapped her knee and pretended to laugh hysterically. Then she threw him an icy glare that said *grow up*. "I filled in the names of the states this morning," she said, "while you were losing whatever you lost." She picked up a blue marker and thrust it in his direction. "You can do the state capitals."

"Lucky me," he mumbled, plucking the marker out of her hand. He opened his backpack and took out an atlas he'd found in his living room. He propped it open on the table and began marking off each state capital. The sunshine streaming through the large kitchen window nearby was a painful reminder of the beautiful afternoon that was going to waste. The only consolation was that he'd found the book and it was safely tucked away in his desk.

Gina got busy adding geographical landmarks to the map, and for the next twenty minutes the only sound to be heard was the squeak of magic markers on the poster board. Gina started to relax a little as she examined her neat writing, scoffing at Nathan's slipshod markings.

At least he's here working on it.

Nathan was still working on the state capitals when Gina asked, "Do you want something to drink? There's soda in the fridge."

"Sure," he said, dropping his marker.

Anything is better than this.

He went to the refrigerator and dug out a can of orange soda. Just as he was opening it he noticed something hanging on the wall. "Hey, my dad has that same calendar."

"Doesn't everyone?" Gina replied without looking up. "They were selling them in every store last Christmas."

"Yeah...I remember..." he said, his voice falling off. For several seconds he stood there without speaking as a thought took shape in the back of his mind.

"What is it?" Gina asked, looking up from the map. He didn't reply. "Nathan?"

"Uh...nothing," he said at last, "just thinking." He walked back over to the table and sat down, but he couldn't focus on school work just yet.

That calendar on the wall.

His dad hung it in his new office, right over the table. It was no big deal when he saw it because...

That's when I found the book.

He dropped the soda can on the floor, sending a spray of orange soda across the porcelain tile.

"HEY, what are you doing?" Gina yelled, jumping up from the table. She ran over to the counter to grab paper towels while Nathan sat and stared out the window, lost in thought. When Gina came back seconds later, she thrust a roll of paper towels at him. "Here, YOU clean it up."

Nathan ignored her and the paper towels. "There's something I have to check out," he said as he stood up and walked away from the table.

"What are you talking about? COME CLEAN THIS UP."

He said nothing as he left the kitchen and walked like a zombie down the hallway towards the front door.

"NATHAN!"

She hastily cleaned the floor and rushed outside after him. She had to run to catch up and managed to reach him just as he was rounding the far corner of his house. "Where are you going?" she insisted, slightly out of breath. But Nathan never answered or even acknowledged her as he continued along the side of the house. He went to the side door—the same one he and his Dad used to bring in the new file cabinet.

When they stepped inside, his father was nowhere to be seen. The room was dark and quiet, so he went over to the desk and turned on the lamp. A soft white light immediately filled the room. Then he turned around.

"Are you going to tell me what's going on...?" Gina began.

"Just as I thought," Nathan said, ignoring her question. He was looking at the calendar on the wall. "It's the same one that..." His mouth stopped working mid-sentence, and for a moment he stood there frozen in place, unable to speak.

"What?" Gina asked.

His attention was drawn to the table that sat directly beneath the calendar. His jaw hung open, as if the words he wanted to say were stuck sideways in his throat. Sitting on the table was the book—the same one he'd hidden in his desk drawer less than an hour before.

"What's going on?" Gina asked. "You look like you've seen a ghost."

Ghost.

The moment she said the word, it all came together in his mind: the attic, the breathing noise, the pages turning and now a second appearance in the basement. It wasn't a trick book—it was something very different. He just didn't want to admit it.

"Ghost..." he whispered, as thoughts began to churn in his mind.

40

It couldn't be.
But it fit.
I heard it.
A ripple of fear shot through his body.
The book took a breath.
He felt his legs getting weak...
Then the pages turned all by themselves.
And his knees started to buckle.
It wouldn't stay on the shelf.
He grabbed the edge of the desk to steady himself.
It's a haunted book.

By now he was clinging to the edge of the desk to keep from falling on the floor. Gina looked at his horror-stricken face, and then she gazed over at the wall. All she saw was the calendar, and just below it—the table. There was an old book lying there but nothing else. It didn't make any sense.

"Nathan...NATHAN...what's wrong?" she asked, shaking his rigid body. "Is it that book?" She started for the table when he reached out and grabbed her arm.

"NO!" he shouted, breaking out of his trance. The signs had been there from the very start, right before his eyes, but for some reason he didn't see them.

Didn't want to see them.

"Don't go near it," he told her in a voice that was calm and calculating. Through it all, he never took his eyes from the book.

Gina didn't know what to do. Nathan had never acted like this before. Whatever he knew he wasn't telling her, and that only made the situation more confusing. Why the fuss over a simple book? Or was it the calendar? Her answer came seconds later when the front cover of the book flipped open and pages started to turn, one by one. The sight of it made her flinch, but then she let out a long breath and shook her head in disbelief.

"OK, very funny," she said. "You got me. Ha. Ha."

Now it was making sense. This was classic Nathan Cole. He had somehow rigged the book to open and for the pages to turn all by themselves. Probably just a small fan, hidden out of sight, or a piece of fishing line, invisible to the eye. She made another move towards the book, but he grabbed her arm and pulled her back a second time.

"Seriously Nathan. You got me. It was very clever but can we *please* go finish our project?"

Nathan held her back as he continued staring at the book. "No," he said in the same flat voice as the realization sank in. He knew from the start that the book was 'different,' but he didn't know how or why. Did he even believe in ghosts? He wasn't sure—not until now.

"At least tell me how you did it. I mean, it was very convincing."

Nathan didn't respond. He ran his left hand through the long hair that was hanging in his face, slowly pushing it back over his ear as he continued to stare at the book. "Stay here," he said as he stood up.

Gina knew that move. She'd seen him do it dozens of times, like when he was about to do one of his stupid bike tricks. It was a nervous tick, and he always did it just before he took action.

"Wait," she said, as he moved away from the desk. "What are you going to do?"

He ignored her question and took a step towards the table, eyes dead ahead. The things he'd seen made perfect sense now.

"I know what you are," he said in a stone cold voice.

"Who are you talking to?" Gina asked, looking around.

He took another step as each of the bizarre events flashed through his mind. "You have something to tell me, don't you?"

"Uh...Nathan? Hello?" Gina said, wishing he'd stop this crazy talk. It was giving her goose bumps up and down both arms.

"What is it you want?" Nathan said, moving closer.

"Nathan!"

"It's ok," he said in that same eerie tone. "It wants us to look."

"*Who* wants...?" she began to say as he moved closer to the table. "Look? Look at *what?*"

But he didn't answer. His full attention remained on the book with steel sharp focus. "Just tell me what you want," he said softly as he continued to move forward in measured steps. Gina was calling to him but he couldn't hear her. In his mind there was no one else in the room. There was only the book. "You've been trying to tell me all along, haven't you?"

His movements were slow and steady, and as he continued to move his voice remained low and reassuring. "I wasn't paying attention..." He was very close now. "But you wouldn't let up."

Gina wanted to run after him and pull him back, but her legs felt like they were bound in plaster. Even if she could, she didn't think it would do any good; Nathan was in some kind of a trance, possessed even, mumbling strange things in that creepy voice. It was way beyond any measure of determination he'd ever shown—all because of a book.

But that didn't make any sense—Nathan Cole hated books. Then another possibility dawned on her and it sent a ripple of fear through her entire body.

Maybe it isn't a trick after all.
He was just reaching for the book when she screamed.
   "NATHAN...DON'T!"

Chapter Three

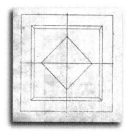

Raven

He was inches from the book. But just as he was about to touch it his hand shot upwards and he plucked the calendar off the wall. Gina stood frozen in place back near the desk, not sure what would happen next.

"It's got to be in here somewhere," he said as he threw back the cover of the calendar. His voice was back to normal, which offered Gina a small amount of comfort.

"What's got to be there?" she asked.

And do I really want to know?

He didn't answer. He was too busy poring over the pages, studying the photographs and the captions for each month. He also checked his father's handwriting, a collection of scribbles on various days of the month and in the margins. There were company names, contacts, meeting times and locations, and not much else—nothing to explain why the book had mysteriously appeared in this room. Twice. "Nothing," he said, shaking his head in disgust. "There's nothing here."

"What are you talking about?"

He looked down at the calendar in his hands for several long seconds.

Just tell her...maybe she can help.

Then he let out a long breath. "OK," he said, walking back to the desk. "I'll tell you...but you're not going to believe it."

"Believe what?"

He told her about the box of old dishes and his visit to the attic, the book hitting the floor and the breathing sound. He recounted the strange events he'd witnessed in his bedroom, the book opening and pages turning all by themselves, and how it completely disappeared. Then he explained how he found it in the basement, right near the calendar—the same calendar that was hanging in her kitchen.

"...And that's when I knew the calendar had to be connected to the book, and all the crazy things it's been doing."

Gina stood there with a look of sheer astonishment on her face, mortified by what she'd just heard.

"What's wrong?" he asked.

"What's wrong?" she repeated. "I don't know what's going on here, but you need to put that book back in the attic where you found it. Right away."

"I tried to," he said, looking sheepishly at the floor, "but it wouldn't let me."

"Wouldn't LET you? It's...a...BOOK," she shouted.

"Yeah...well...for some reason..."

"STOP IT," she said before he could finish. "It's always some excuse with you. Just take it back up there and leave it. Let's go back to my house and…"

"You don't believe me," he interrupted, throwing his hands in the air with a sigh. The calendar went sailing over his shoulder and landed on the floor.

"I don't know *what* to believe," she fired back. She folded her arms and turned away. The room fell quiet for several long seconds.

"Look," Nathan said, breaking the stalemate, "I didn't know what to believe either, until right now. Don't you see? This is the second time today that I found the book on that table. That has to mean something."

"Why?" she shot back, turning around to face him. "Why does it being on the table have to mean anything?"

"Because of the calendar. It's linked to the book somehow."

"How do you figure that?"

"Because it's the only thing nearby."

"What are you talking about? There's lots of other stuff in this room..."

"Exactly," he replied, cutting her off, "but the book wasn't near any of it. Not the desk, not the computer, not the shelf. It was right below the calendar."

Gina rolled her eyes and let out a breath. "OK, Mr. Conspiracy, I'll prove to you that none of this means anything. You said you found the book on your desk, and it was open, right?"

"That's right."

"Did you read what was on the page?"

"Uh...no...when I picked it up the pages started turning, so I threw it down on the desk. Then I closed it."

"You closed it?" *That was dumb.*

"Yeah, it scared me, so I closed it." *Like you wouldn't have done the same thing.*

"But it opened up again?"

"Yes..."

"And did you read what was on the page that time?"

"Yeah, I read the whole chapter."

"And did it have anything to do with calendars?"

"No," he said. "Here, I'll show you."

He walked back over to the table and was about to pick up the book when he stopped short and stared at the open pages. When he looked back at Gina his face was pale, like he wanted to say something but his jaw was wired in place.

"What is it this time?" she asked.

He didn't say a word, he just motioned with his hand.

"No way," she said, refusing to fall for another one of his tricks. "Just tell me."

But Nathan shook his head and motioned again.

Gina exhaled loudly and then said, "All right, I'll come over there and look at...*whatever*...then I'm out of here." She walked cautiously over to where he was standing and gave the page a cursory glance. "OK...what about it?"

That's when he finally turned to her and spoke. It was in that same calm voice, the one that gave her the chills all over.

"He wants us to read this."

Gina looked around. "He? Who are you talking about?"

He turned back to the book. Using his index finger he gently tapped on the faded picture in the top corner of the page.

Gina looked down at the photo. It was faint, but even so the man looked half-crazed. It was the black suit and slicked down hair that looked like it was glued to his head. And with a name like that, who *wouldn't* think he was crazy? Alastair Raven.

It was the same picture of Raven that Nathan saw when the book reopened on his desk. Moments earlier when he saw it, for the second time, he realized that it wasn't a coincidence. That's when all the pieces fell into place.

The same chapter.

It was that picture of Raven...

The same page.

That first got his attention.

I picked it up.

And got him reading.

But I never finished.

Then he fell asleep.

I never saw what he wanted me to see.

But now it all made sense.

"What are you saying?" Gina asked, staring the picture of Raven. "*He's* making the book do this?" She rubbed her arms, trying to fight off the chill that was making her tremble.

Nathan slowly nodded his head. His eyes were fixed on hers, and his expression was dead serious.

Gina stepped back from the table and threw up her hands. "OK, that's it." She shook her head in disbelief as she spoke. "Now I've heard everything."

Without another word she turned and stormed out the door.

Nathan made no move to slow her down or stop her. If she didn't believe him, so be it. This was real, he was sure of it now—Raven was reaching out to him, leading him to something. But what? He hung up the calendar on the wall—it could wait until later. "I need to read this chapter again," he whispered, closing the book and tucking it under his arm. It was what he was supposed to do from the start—that much was clear to him now.

49

He went straight upstairs to his room, closed the door and began reading. This time, sleep would not overtake him—something was buried in the musty pages of the old book and he was determined to find it. As he stared at the fuzzy picture of Alastair Raven and read his date of birth, he was overcome with a burning question.

What could a man who lived over 150 years ago possibly want me to know?

♦

Gina mumbled to herself the whole way home. He had some nerve, trying to trick her like that.

Just to get out of studying, I'll bet.

Then again, this was Nathan Cole. He'd been her neighbor for as long as she could remember, and he was always up to something. The more she thought about it the faster she walked.

"A flying book..." she said, kicking at the grass as she stormed across the lawn. "Pages that turn by themselves. What a bunch of baloney."

It was some kind of trick. It had to be. And to top it off, he never did tell her how he got the book to do all those crazy things.

She marched back to her house and straight into the kitchen to gather her art supplies. The map project could wait. They still had a few days to finish it, and if Nathan Cole thought she was going to do it all by herself, well, he was seriously mistaken.

With her art supplies and the map put away, she turned her attention to more relaxing matters—a book of puzzles. It was one of many she kept around the house for moments like this, and in no time at all she was curled up on the couch, totally absorbed in a tricky cryptogram. "Let's see you try to figure this out, Nathan Cole." The thought of it made her laugh out loud.

A short time later she got hungry and went into the kitchen for a snack. On her way to the refrigerator she saw the calendar hanging on the wall. "Oh look, it's the missing link," she said and then chuckled. She got an apple and went back to her puzzle. "Like I'd fall for that."

Three cryptograms and two word search puzzles later, she still hadn't gotten over Nathan's failed attempt to trick her. He'd worked so hard to pull it off, but she was smarter than he was. And not nearly as gullible as he wanted to believe. It was one of his better performances, though, she'd give him that. Just to prove to herself that he was wrong and she was right, she decided to take a look at the calendar. He'd never know, and then she'd drop the whole thing once and for all.

She went back to the kitchen and took the calendar off the wall. She had totally ignored it since her mother first hung it up, but as she looked through it now the beauty of the pictures amazed her. There were rustic barns, rolling meadows blanketed with bright yellow daisies and elegant flower gardens bursting with color along fancy tiled walkways. Two photos in particular stood out—a multicolored sunset shimmering over a peaceful Adirondack lake and ribbons of Texas Bluebonnets lining both sides of an old railroad bed.

She carefully examined every picture, trying to find some small detail that might fit—all the while seeing the faded picture of Alastair Raven in the back of her mind. Because she knew almost nothing about him, other than the fact that he lived a long time ago, she had no idea what information might be significant. She studied each of the pictures with the expectation that there was a hidden clue there, one that Nathan had missed.

When she was done with the photos, she checked for any holidays or seasonal events. Perhaps they'd named a special day or a celebration after him. Maybe there was some historical tidbit that had to do with him. Anything was possible. She checked and rechecked all twelve months, but Raven's name was nowhere to be seen. She even checked the local advertising at the bottom of each page. When she was done, she went back to the beginning and started over again, just to be sure.

After examining and re-examining every page, she finally called it quits and hung the calendar back on the wall in the kitchen. There wasn't a single mention of Alastair Raven anywhere, or anything else for that matter, that could even remotely be connected with the book. Any book.

"Some link," she laughed, as she went back to her puzzle book. The whole calendar idea was a complete waste of time, which made her laugh even more. It proved that the joke was on Nathan—he just didn't know it yet.

Nathan read like he never had before, soaking in every word and every picture.

Alastair Raven was born to wealthy parents in Cambridge, Massachusetts in 1825. Because of his family's wealthy status, he was sent to the finest schools of the day where he excelled in math and science. From his earliest years it became obvious to those around him, especially his teachers, that his true calling was design.

His keen eye and artistic flair showed great promise. When he finished school, he began an apprenticeship with an architectural master named Franklin Jarratt, who trained him in the art of building. Jarratt had completed *his* apprenticeship with Richard Morris Hunt—one of New York City's most renowned architects, and a man whose style had graced everything from factories and warehouses, to schools, hospitals and railroad stations. Before long, however, it was Raven's designs that began to emerge throughout the city.

As his designs grew in popularity, so did Alastair Raven. He was the speaker of choice at corporate meetings and college lectures. His name began to appear at the top of the guest list for every social gala and private party. With his designs dotting the landscape of the growing city, people suddenly wanted to know the man, live in his shadow and bask in the glow of his success.

Nathan lingered on the pages with photos, tracing them with his finger. As he read, he was impressed by the examples of Raven's work. There were detailed sketches of arcades and porticos, elaborate bargeboards and decorative brackets. Gradually the drawings became more complex and Nathan began to see triple arched windows, decorative cornices, steep gables and intricately carved finials, each drawn in remarkable detail. It was obvious by the drawings that Raven had both an extreme talent and passion for what he did. But that's where the story took a mysterious turn.

And that's when he found it.

It was the one detail that explained all the peculiar things the book had done. They didn't seem so bizarre, or scary, because now he understood that each of them was meant to get his attention.

Get him to read.

To see.

One word.

Chapter Four

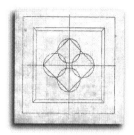

AV

Vanished.

In 1862, at the height of his career, Alastair Raven simply disappeared. In what was considered the strangest missing persons case of its time, one of the great architectural masters of the 19th century was gone without a trace.

There was no motive. There were no clues. The authorities investigated it from every angle but came up empty-handed each time. The man had simply ceased to exist. And because he had no surviving family, no grieving wife or children to push the investigation, it eventually stalled. To this day it was still officially listed as unsolved.

Friends and members of the architectural community were outraged, but the police simply had nothing to go on. No crime had been committed, and although his work would stand for decades to come, Alastair Raven would never be heard from again.

Until now. The thought sent a shiver through Nathan's body and he shifted in the chair.

He's reaching out to me...

His train of thought was broken when he heard someone calling his name.

"NATHAN?...DINNER."

He checked the clock on his bedside table. He had been reading for nearly three hours—a new Nathan Cole World Record. But it left him with even more questions. The book led him to this point, but what did it mean? What was it that Raven wanted him to find? Those questions haunted him through dinner and well into his dreams that night.

The next morning, Nathan sauntered out to the bus stop, preoccupied with a growing list of nagging questions. Gina was waiting on the sidewalk, watching for the bus, and never saw him cut across the lawn behind her.

"Hey," he grunted.

She jumped at the sound, dropping her backpack. "DON'T DO THAT," she snarled.

"Sorry," he said, unable to keep from laughing.

She scooped up her backpack with an angry swipe and turned her back to him.

That was it—now she definitely wasn't going to tell him about the calendar. Let him waste more time on his foolish notion.

Then we'll see who's laughing.

During last block Gina was in the library, working at one of the long tables. Nathan came walking over and she didn't notice him until he pulled up a chair and sat down beside her. In his hands was a large book that he plunked down on the table with a thud that echoed across the room. Without a word he opened it up and started scanning the pages.

She did her best to ignore him, but something about this didn't add up. He was completely focused on reading—a book, of all things.

Seriously? Nathan Cole? Reading?

She turned her head and twirled a strand of hair behind her ear, casually looking in his direction.

What is he so interested in?

The book was too far away, so she flipped her pencil into the air and it flew sideways, hitting his arm. "Oh sorry," she giggled, but Nathan was too busy reading to notice. She slowly reached over to pick it up, taking time to scan everything on the page. Staring back at her was the same faded picture of Alastair Raven that she'd seen in Nathan's basement. The very sight of the man gave her goose bumps all over again.

Is that the only picture they have of that guy?

She shuddered and quickly picked up her pencil, then went back to her own work.

Nathan studied the page for some time and then turned to the next, examining every word, every picture with the utmost concentration. Gina pretended not to notice what he was doing, but every now and then she'd sneak a casual glance his way.

Nathan reached the bottom of the page and looked up at the clock on the wall. "Whoa, time to go," he said, quickly closing the book. Just as he got up from his chair, Gina stopped what she was doing and looked up from the table. She stared across the room with a blank expression on her face, as if there were something on the far wall that she was trying to read.

"Nathan?" she said calmly.

He had already started to walk away and never saw the change come over her. Until he turned around.

"Yeah?"

"Wait."

She was sitting completely still, like her entire body had been dipped in wax.

"What's wrong?"

"Can I have a look at that book?"

"Uh...sure," he said, studying the blank look on her face. He walked back to the table and that's when she snapped out of her trance. She turned and looked at him with a mystified look on her face.

"Show me what you were reading."

"Yeah, no problem," he said slowly. He set the book down on the table, watching her face the whole time. Clearly something had spooked her. She never took her eyes from the book as he opened it up and began turning pages. When he found the chapter he'd been reading he slid the book towards her.

"I need to check something," she said, pulling it closer.

"Take your time," he said, watching the expression on her face as she carefully inspected each page. Alastair Raven had built numerous buildings, many of which were pictured in the book, but one of them held her attention for a full minute. She studied it closely and then her eyes dropped to the caption just below the photo.

"Polk County Courthouse, Colfax, Virginia, 1852."

Before Nathan could ask her what was so special about that photo, she abruptly picked up the book and walked away from the table. "Where are you...?" he began to ask, both palms open in a *what gives* gesture. But she just kept walking and he jumped up from the chair. "Wait for me."

She lugged the book over to the photocopier and was just positioning it on the scanner glass when he arrived.

"What are you *doing?*" His curiosity was on full alert.

"Making a copy."

"No...really? Like I didn't already..."

"Shhh."

She watched the photocopy slowly feed out of the side of the machine and then picked it up and gave it a quick inspection.

"What is it?" he pleaded.

She folded the paper and said, "A possible link."

"Just tell me," Nathan insisted, a short time later as he followed Gina out to the bus.

"I will...when we get home," she replied. "How many times do I have to say it?"

"But why not *now?*"

She stopped walking and turned to face him. She didn't even know why she was doing this. "Because I'm not sure, OK? It's just a hunch."

And if I'm wrong you'll never let me hear the end of it.

"How about just a small clue?" he said, gesturing with his thumb and forefinger. If she had information about the book, he wanted to know it, now.

She exhaled loudly. "You know something...?" she started to say. Patience had never been one of Nathan Cole's strong suits.

"What?" he asked defensively.

She took a deep breath and then griped, "Oh never mind." She made an abrupt turn and climbed up the stairs of the bus.

He didn't ask her again after that.

When they got home, Gina made a beeline across the lawn towards her house, with Nathan following close behind. Silently. She went straight into the kitchen, dropped her backpack on a chair, and then headed to the refrigerator for a drink.

"No soda for you," she said, taking a can of ginger ale off the door.

"How come?" he whined.

She opened the can and took a long thirst-quenching sip.

"Is this about yesterday?"

She continued to ignore him as she walked over and pulled the calendar off the wall. He immediately sat up in the chair. "What are you doing with that?"

"You'll see." She brought the calendar over to the table.

"Wait a minute...did you...?"

"Quiet," she said, handing him the soda can. He took one look at it and scoffed, then quickly set it aside as she placed the calendar on the table and flipped to the back.

"What's that?" he asked, moving closer.

"October."

"No kidding."

She pointed to the bottom of the page and then began fishing through her backpack.

"What's this supposed to be?" he asked, casually glancing at the large banner that ran across the bottom of the page.

"An advertisement."

"Gee thanks...I'm pretty sure I figured that out already."

She pulled the photocopy out of her backpack. "Very funny. Now move over."

He exhaled loudly and moved aside as she sat down and put the photocopy of the library book next to the calendar. Then she leaned forward and began to examine each one very carefully. Nathan craned his neck, trying to see what she was looking at, but her head was blocking his view. This went on for some time until he couldn't stand it any longer. "An advertisement for what?"

"Owens Hardware," she answered without looking up. "It's their 75th anniversary."

"Big deal."

"Probably is," she replied, trying her best to tune him out. Her full attention was on the advertisement, which included a photo of Owens Hardware on the day it opened for business.

"What is it?" Nathan asked impatiently.

She stood up and said, "See for yourself."

He sat down and considered the advertisement briefly and then shrugged.

"There," she said, directing him to the left side of the photo. It was taken from the far end of the street and from that angle, the front of another building was visible. She could hardly contain her excitement.

"See it?" Gina asked.

"Yeah...this building on the corner...the front entrance..."

"It looks like the one in the photocopy, right?"

Nathan looked over at the photocopy, then back to the advertisement. "They do look similar...but these pictures are pretty fuzzy."

"Hold on." She quickly dug into her backpack and pulled out an old wood-handled magnifying glass.

"You carry a magnifying glass in your backpack? Who are you, Sherlock Holmes?"

"No...I took it to school for..." she began. "Do you want to use it or not?"

"Yes...please," he said in a syrupy voice. *Sherlock.*

She hesitated and then handed it to him. *Clown.*

He moved in close and began scrutinizing both pictures, comparing every detail as if committing them to memory.

"Well?" she asked.

"They don't just look alike," he said, his face inches from the photo. He sat up, a look of utter shock on his face. "They're identical."

"Are you sure?" There was a measure of doubt in her voice.

He nodded. "Here, I'll show you."

She stepped closer as he positioned the magnifying glass above the photocopy.

"See this pointed arch? It's called an ogee arch."

"OK."

"And these fancy designs in the top corners? They're called spandrels."

"If you say so."

He went back to the photo in the advertisement, holding the magnifying glass just inches above it. "Have a look."

She leaned in close and studied the photo intently. Then she stood up, with the same look of astonishment she'd just seen on his face. "You're right...they're the same."

"How did you know?" he asked, eyeing her suspiciously.

"Know what?"

"About the picture in the calendar?"

"I...um...noticed it..." she said casually, looking away. "When? You never looked at it in my dad's office. In fact, *you* said..."

"All right, all right," she blurted out. "I came home and looked at it after I left your house."

Nathan slowly nodded his head. "And you saw that other picture in the book I was reading in the library."

"Well...I peeked...just a little," she confessed.

"When you threw your pencil at me." It wasn't a question. She tried to hide a guilty smile.

"You know what that means?" He was about to burst.

Here we go, she thought.

"You did it!" he exclaimed, catching her off guard. "This is the link. It explains why the book was on the table in my dad's office."

The very thought gave her the chills all over again.

"I can't believe you found it."

"Hey, don't sound so surprised," she said in an offended voice.

"I'm not...it's just...what I mean is...you are SO awesome."

"Well of course," she said, blushing.

Now that you mention it.

He set the magnifying glass down on the table and glanced at his watch. It was almost 3:30 p.m.

"What's the matter?" she asked.

"Nothing. Do you want to take a ride?"

"A ride? What are you talking about?"

"Come on," he said, grabbing the photocopy from the table.

"Wait...where are we going?"

"There," he replied, pointing to the advertisement. Ten minutes later they were on their bikes and headed into town.

♦

Owens Hardware wasn't hard to find. It took up every square inch of the street except for the lot on the corner. That space was occupied by a monstrous vine-covered building—the same in the calendar photo.

"Wow, Gina said as she stared up at the towering structure. There was no other word to describe it.

"You can say that again," Nathan answered. "Come on."

They left their bikes on the sidewalk and climbed up the massive front steps for a closer look.

"You know what's weird?" Gina asked when they reached the top step. "I don't remember this building being here."

"Me neither," Nathan replied. "But do you ever come down here...to this part of town?"

"Nope."

"Exactly," he said, turning his attention back to the building. Many of the architectural details were locked in his memory after reading the book. Up close they were even more spectacular. "Dripstone," he whispered, staring up at the second floor of the building. His expression was a mix of confidence and awe.

"What did you say?""See those hood moldings on the windows?"

"Hood...what?"

"Hood moldings...up there...at the top of the windows."

"OK," she said, looking intently at a window on the second floor.

"They're called dripstone. They throw off the rain."

She turned and stared at Nathan for a long moment without speaking.

It looks like him. It sounds like him. Since when did he...

"It all fits," he said, nodding his head.

"What do you mean? Fits what?"

"Let's go," he said as he turned and hurried back down the steps. "There's something I need to find out."

How did Nathan Cole suddenly know everything before her?

"Wait..." she shouted, but he was already on his bike and peddling down the sidewalk towards Owens Hardware. By the time she caught up to him he was already off his bike and walking towards the front door.

"Will you WAIT?" she yelled as she leaned her bike up against the front wall of the store.

Owens Hardware was a huge store, but when they walked in they only saw one employee—a short older man with thin gray hair. He was standing behind the front counter bagging a customer's order.

Gina took one look and stopped walking. The man was wearing a blue apron splattered and smudged with different colors of paint. His thick wire-framed glasses made his eyes look bigger than normal.

Mr. Thonis?...from science class?

Mr. Thonis was a big fan of the apron, even on the days when they weren't doing some bizarre experiment and nearly burning down the school. She wondered if this lookalike would be more patient and less prone to shouting.

When he saw them come through the door, the man stopped what he was doing long enough to say, "Sorry kids, we're all done with donations. Try me next year." Then he turned back to the customer, shaking his head while he spoke. "It never ends. I swear there's a kid in here every day, looking for a handout."

The customer shot a quick glance over his shoulder at Nathan and Gina, then took his purchase and hurried out the door. The man in the blue apron grumbled something under his breath, picked up a clipboard and then padded over to the paint section.

"Come on," Nathan whispered to Gina. He started to walk in that direction.

65

"Wait," she blurted out, grabbing his arm and pulling him back. "What are you doing?"

"Don't worry...just follow me."

"Nathan!" she pleaded, but he pulled away from her and kept walking.

The man in the blue apron was standing in the paint aisle, closely inspecting a row of paint cans up on the shelf. When he found the one he wanted, he took it down and started back up the aisle. That's when he noticed Nathan standing near the paint brush display.

"Very busy today, son," he said as he hoisted the gallon of paint up on the workbench. "Lots of paint to mix." He consulted his clipboard momentarily and was reaching for a pry tool to open the can when he knocked over a large container of paint stirrers. "Well that's just perfect." He groaned as they tumbled to the floor with a clatter. Nathan quickly moved in and gathered them up.

"Thanks," the man said with a surprised look. "You don't see many people do that these days. Help out, I mean."

"No problem," Nathan said, handing him the bundle. He noticed the name *Ken* embroidered in red stitching on the front pocket of the apron.

Ken saw him reading it and said, "Ken Owens, store owner, nice to meet you."

"Nathan Cole." Then he quickly added, "I'm not here for a donation. I just came in to ask you about the building on the corner."

"The building on the corner? You mean the old courthouse?"

Courthouse? As soon as he heard the word, Nathan felt a jolt of nervous excitement. "Uh...yeah...I didn't know that's what it was." From several feet away, he heard Gina clear her throat. "Oh, sorry, this is my friend Gina."

Ken gave her a quick nod. "What is it you want to know?"

"Do you have any idea when it was built?" Nathan asked.

"Well...let's see..." Ken said. "I think it was back around the turn of the century, maybe a little earlier."

"Do you know *who* built it?" Gina chimed in.

"Well," Ken said, "that's a very good question. I can't say I ever knew, strange as that is, but I imagine they keep that sort of thing on file down at the Town Hall."

Nathan checked his watch. It was almost 4:30 p.m. He was wondering if the Town Hall stayed open this late when Ken added, "You know...I do seem to remember something about the builder's name."

Nathan froze.

Say it. Say it.

"It's not much, but I remember it had a V in it." He looked down at the floor, thinking intently. "Oh what was that name?"

"Would it be listed inside the building, like, on a plaque or something?" Gina asked.

"It's possible," Ken said, "but how are you going to get inside to see it? That building hasn't been used in years. The doors are all locked."

Nathan frowned. "Locked?"

"That's right. Ever since they built that new courthouse across town."

"You were saying something about the builder's name?" Nathan asked.

"Right," Ken replied. He looked down at the floor again, scratching the side of his head as he tried to remember.

As the seconds ticked away, it became clear that he wasn't going to dredge it up from his memory anytime soon.

"You know," he said, "you could always check the front of the building. He put his initials on it…"

Almost instantly, Nathan and Gina turned and raced towards the door.

"THANKS," Nathan shouted as he pushed through the door.

"YEAH…THANK YOU," Gina yelled as she followed him out.

"HOLD ON," he called to them. "THERE'S MORE…" But it was no use. Nathan and Gina had already climbed on their bikes and were gone. "Take a good look," he said to the empty store as he went back to work. "It won't be there for long."

Nathan and Gina rode back to the corner. They parked their bikes at the foot of the steps and then raced up them towards the entrance. When they were almost to the top, they stopped and looked up, searching the front of the building from top to bottom.

"There," Nathan said, pointing to a small horizontal slab of stone built into the front of the building below the peak.

It was just two letters.

Neither of them said a word. They stared at the nameplate for a full minute as the reality of the situation sank in.

Someone had built this amazing structure, but it wasn't Alastair Raven.

Slowly, Nathan's shoulders drooped. "It can't be," he whispered. "It just can't..."

One by one, the entire chain of events that led them to this moment began to unravel in his mind, until all he had left was questions. If Raven wasn't the builder, why did the book lead them to the basement? Was he wrong about the calendar? Was there something else he was supposed to see?

Impossible.

He felt defeated. But this had to be it. The calendar was the only thing that made sense. Just as he had explained to Gina, it was the only thing near the book. Then she found the courthouse picture in the calendar and he felt it all coming together. They were on to something. But now, as he stood on the courthouse steps, the simplicity of their failure disgusted him. Two lousy letters—that's all it took to blow his theory out of the water.

"Unbelievable," he muttered, shaking his head.

"What?"

"This," he said, motioning to the building before them. "It was all a waste of time."

Gina saw the broken look on his face. "Come on, we better go."

They walked slowly down the steps to the street and climbed on their bikes. As they rode away, Nathan was too angry to look back. He just wanted to forget the whole thing.

When they got back home, they stopped at the end of Nathan's driveway.

"Well, thanks for help," he told Gina. "I'm sorry I wasted your time."

"That's OK," she replied. In a curious change of heart, she actually felt bad for him. Ever since they left the library, she was sure she'd found the link between the book and the calendar. All it took to convince her was tangible proof. Something real.

"I gotta go," he said, "I'll see you tomorrow."

"Yeah, talk to you then."

Nathan rode up the driveway and parked his bike behind the house. The anger he felt earlier was now replaced with feelings of disappointment. For a short time it felt like they were on to something big. An amazing adventure—one that ended just as it was getting started.

"Did you have a good day, Nathan?" his mother asked him during dinner.

"Yeah," he mumbled, staring at his spaghetti. It looked like he was eating a bird's nest with two large meatballs in it.

"Is school going OK?"

"Fine." Or maybe a flattened ball of yarn with two meaty eyes.

When he was finished he went up to his room to do his homework. Normally he dreaded this part of the day, but at least it would take his mind off the wasted trip downtown with Gina.

As he sat at his desk working, he could hear his parents laughing downstairs in the kitchen. Somewhere off in the distance there was the whine of a police siren. An airplane flew over the house.

Then he heard something else.

It was a noise he couldn't identify, coming from somewhere outside his bedroom window. At first it was very faint and he ignored it, but then he heard it again. Louder this time. He stopped reading.

What is that?

It was some kind of soft rumbling sound, and he looked up from his school book, listening intently.

There it is again...

Closer.

Something was shaking and it wasn't outside his window—it was here—in the room. He spun around to see what was.

And jumped out of his chair.

Chapter Five

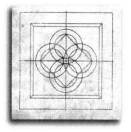

Vasari

"HEY!" He jumped up and sprinted across the room, reaching his bedside table just in time to grab his lamp before it fell on the floor. His alarm clock was sliding off the opposite edge, so he quickly leaned over and snagged that too. As he set them down on the bed, he noticed the book was the only thing on the table that wasn't headed to the floor. It just sat there vibrating, causing the whole table to shake uncontrollably. That explained the noise he heard.

But why was it...?

Before he could finish his thought, the book flipped open. It was just like before. Same chapter. Same page. But this time he didn't flinch or freeze; he felt his anger boil to the surface.

"WHAT DO YOU WANT NOW?"

His answer came instantly as one of the images on the page began a startling transformation. The steel gray ink warmed to a soft pink and then to bright red. At the same time it began to pulsate like a glowing ember. Nathan rubbed his eyes. He recognized the image immediately; it was similar to the photo he'd seen in the calendar and almost a perfect match of the one he'd seen in-person earlier in the day—the entryway to the courthouse. He felt his anger surging once again and, grabbing the book, he flung it across the table with a vicious sweep of his hand.

"YOU'RE WRONG."

The book bounced harmlessly off his bureau and landed on the floor. Then it flipped open again. This time the image grew even brighter and sent a shimmering column of crimson light up to the ceiling.

"NO," he growled through clenched teeth as he went over and kicked the book shut with his foot. He started to pull his foot away when the book suddenly opened again. He kicked it shut again but got the same result. After a third attempt he finally gave up. "I DON'T CARE, OK?"

He turned around and went back to his desk, but that's when the beam of light began to change again. It grew wider and wider with each passing second, radiating outward and eventually filling the entire room with a blinding red haze.

"STOP!" he pleaded, turning away, but it was so overwhelming that he was forced to cover his eyes with both hands. In one last desperate attempt to make it stop, he stumbled over to his bed and ripped off the covers, balling them up in his arms. Then he stumbled across the room and dumped them in a heap on top of the book. Only then was he able to open his eyes again.

Early the next morning when Gina left for school, she found Nathan sitting on her front steps. She had barely opened the door when he jumped to his feet.

"It's him," he blurted out.

74

"What?" she asked.

"Last night...in the book..." he began.

"Wait, wait, wait," she said, cutting him off. "I thought we were finished with all that. You *do* remember what happened yesterday afternoon, right?"

This wasn't the reaction he was expecting. Before he could counter, she pushed past him and walked down the steps towards the sidewalk. At the far end of the street, the school bus was just rounding the corner. He turned and hurried after her, trying to think of what to say.

"OK...forget I said that," he called out, "but listen...there's one more thing we need to do."

"One more thing *we* need to do?" she said sarcastically, without turning around. "And just what might that be?"

The bus pulled up to the curb and stopped a few feet from where they were standing. The door opened and she stepped inside.

"You remember at the hardware store, what Ken said about the courthouse?" he said, following her up the steps into the bus. He had to speak loudly to be heard over the rattle of the diesel engine.

"Of course. I was there with you, remember?"

"Yeah, that was great," he replied, "thanks for doing that, by the way."

She paused at the top step and gave him one of her *nice try* faces. Then she turned and made her way down the center aisle.

"Anyway..." he continued, "Ken said the information about the courthouse was kept down at the Town Hall."

"Yes, that's exactly what he said," Gina confirmed, sitting down in the first empty seat she saw. Nathan plopped down beside her as the door closed and the school bus lurched forward.

"We need to check the history of that building…" he yelled over the noise of the bus and the throng of kids who were having shouting matches of their own.

"Why?" Gina asked, cutting him off. "You saw the initials on the building, they were…"

"I know, I know," he said before she could finish. "But there's a link between Raven and that building, I just know there is."

"You just know…" she repeated. The way she said it made it sound much less convincing. Or believable.

Nathan looked down. If only she'd seen what happened in his room: how the book was making the table shake, the glowing image that became a beam of light so strong it nearly blinded him. But she was clearly in no mood to talk about a haunted book.

He raised his head, staring into her eyes. "Look," he said with as much sincerity as he could muster, "I can't tell you *why* I know…but I just do."

She studied his face as the bus chugged through town, rocking and swaying around each corner like a giant sailing ship at sea. She saw the desperate look of truth, a belief so strong that it was pushing him onward, despite any logical reason to do so. It was quite impressive. She admired his passion, even though nothing they'd found thus far connected Raven to anything.

"When would we go?" she asked. What harm could there be in going to the Town Hall? *As a friend. To humor him.*

"After school."

"Just downtown and back?" They'd probably just talk to some clerk, look at some old documents and then leave.

76

"Yup," he confirmed as the bus eased into the school driveway.

"And we'll be home before dinner?"

"By five, just like last night."

Gina mulled it over in her head as the bus came to a stop and the other kids began to file out. Nathan didn't move either—he had one more salvo. The clincher.

He let out a long breath. "Here's the deal. If it turns out to be another dead end, I promise I'll drop it, once and for all."

Gina studied his face for a moment and then looked away. The bus was nearly empty as the last of the screaming mob departed and joined the horde of kids pushing their way through the front door of the school.

"You'll drop it?" she asked, turning back to face him. "Not another word?"

"Not even a whisper."

The bus driver was watching them in his visor mirror, drumming his fingers impatiently on the steering wheel.

"Let's go," she said.

His eyes went wide. "To the Town Hall?"

"No, dummy," she said, nodding towards the aisle. "To school."

The bus driver was just turning around in his seat to say something to them when Nathan stood up. He stepped aside to let Gina go first and as she brushed past him she said, "OK, I'll go."

This time he didn't need to ask what she meant.

They didn't speak of it for the rest of the school day. But for Nathan, the more he thought about what happened in his room, the more he began to worry. Pages that turn by themselves are one thing. So is a book that moves around the house. But a light so intense that it nearly blinds you? That's something altogether different.

So violent...

The way it kept radiating.

Like it was angry.

As the day wore on, he became convinced that it meant something bad. The brutal nature of what he'd witnessed could only mean that something dangerous lay in store for him. And there was no one he could turn to for help. There was Gina, but every time he mentioned the book it just made her angry and she'd storm off. She refused to hear a single word about it. If by some odd chance she *did* agree to discuss it with him, he knew exactly what he'd say.

"Gina, I'm nervous."

"Nervous about what?"

"Where this is headed."

"It's probably nothing...that's all it's been so far."

"I know, but what if it's not? What if it turns into something dangerous?"

"Then you should drop it immediately."

"I've tried to but...the book...Raven...they keep pushing me. And yet..."

"And yet...what?"

"There's something to all this...I can feel it...and I can't let it go."

"Then you've got to make a decision."

"That's just it...I can't."

It was a wonderful thought, but he knew it would never happen. He was on his own from here on out, regardless of what happened at the Town Hall...*if* anything happened at the Town Hall. If not, if it was just another dead end, then he'd put the book back in the attic and forget about it—as promised. And he wouldn't feel bad about it, either.

The book pushed. I gave it my all. I came up empty. Move on.

It was as simple as that. To spend any more time chasing useless leads would be a total waste of...

"What do *you* think, Nathan?"

"Huh?"

He awoke from his daydream and realized he was still sitting in math class. Everyone in the room was staring at him.

"I asked if you could solve the equation," Ms. Ballard asked from the front of the room. "I know how much you enjoy them."

There was a scattering of giggles around the room as he looked up at the numbers on the blackboard.

$$\tfrac{1}{2} + 7.5 =$$

He drew a complete blank. Maybe if he'd finished his homework the night before he might have known the answer, but that hadn't happened—he was too busy battling a blinding beam of red light that had overtaken his bedroom. Somehow he didn't think Ms. Ballard would buy that excuse.

"Eight," a soft voice whispered from directly behind him.

Nathan cleared his throat and said, "Uh...eight?"

"Very good," Ms. Ballard said, as she scribbled a new equation on the blackboard.

He let out a nervous breath and decided it was time to open his math book—for the first time in several days.

From across the room, Gina saw him randomly flipping pages.

Try paying attention next time...

He clearly had no idea what lesson they were on.

Or maybe do your homework for a change.

She rolled her eyes in disgust.

Instead of reading that dumb book you found.

Her mood began to brighten when she realized this silly book business would be settled once and for all, after school, when they went downtown. She had agreed to go to the Town House with Nathan as a courtesy, and she'd honor that agreement, but *only* because he agreed to drop the whole thing if they came up short.

And come up short they would.

The courthouse had nothing to do with anything. It was a huge waste of time. But if one quick trip downtown was all it took to convince him, so be it. By this time tomorrow, everything would be back to normal again. The Town Hall records would prove nothing, Nathan would finally give up his silly obsession, and she'd never see that scary book or hear about Alastair Raven ever again. Then maybe they could *finally* finish their school project.

♦

They got to the Town Hall just after 4 p.m. It was Nathan's first time in the monstrous building, and the moment he stepped through the front doors he stopped and looked up. The lobby was breathtaking, with tall sculpted pillars and a high vaulted ceiling. Matching staircases sat on each side and circled upstairs to the second floor. Each had a heavy wooden banister the color of coffee beans.

"Wow," he said, as he stood there taking it all in.

"Come on," Gina said as she pushed past him and walked briskly across the hardwood floor to a flight of white marble steps. Beyond the steps was an arched entryway that led to a maze of town offices, and when Gina got there she paused for a moment.

"Where to now?" Nathan asked.

"I'm not sure," she replied, looking left and right. There was a group of offices on the left, but the door was closed and the lights were off. Straight ahead was a deserted conference room with rows of empty chairs. Just then they heard voices erupt from one of the offices off to the right. "This way."

They walked down an adjoining corridor past the conference room. It led around a corner to another cluster of offices—and the source of the noise.

"Who is that?" Nathan whispered as they stopped outside the only office with lights on.

Gina rolled her eyes. "When are you going to learn how to read?" She pointed to the wall next to the door, to a small wooden plaque with gold letters—Town Clerk.

"Well...I'm telling you, I mailed it," a young woman snarled as she stood at the counter. She was hastily filling out a personal check as her two young kids bounced around the waiting area like twin tornadoes.

"Yes, you already mentioned that," the town clerk replied calmly, "but as I told you, we go through our mail very carefully. If your check was there, we definitely would have..."

"HEY! STOP THAT!" the young woman yelled, glaring at her children, who were yanking brochures out of a nearby display rack and dropping them on the floor. They stopped long enough to grin at one another, but just as they were about to continue, Nathan and Gina walked through the door. That sent them running back to the front counter to their mother, who finished signing the check and flung it

81

across the counter in a huff. She grabbed the two children by the arms and dragged them out of the office, through the muddle of brochures that littered the floor.

The town clerk sighed and calmly put the check in a drawer beneath the counter. Then she looked up at Gina. "My apologies," she said, nodding towards the sound of two screaming kids echoing up and down the hallway.

"Don't worry about it," Gina said with a smirk. "You should hear the kids on my bus."

Nathan had taken the liberty of gathering the brochures off the floor and was busy tucking them into the display.

"Wow, you're moving up in the world," Gina said, trying not to giggle. "First it was paint stirrers, now it's brochures."

"Very funny," he said as he slid the last brochure into its slot.

"Thank you for doing that," the town clerk said when he was finished. "Now, what brings you here today? You're much too young to be registering a car."

"Actually," Nathan said, "we're looking for some information about a building in town."

"What kind of information?"

"We want to know who built it."

"I see," the town clerk replied with a nod of her head. "That kind of information is kept downstairs in our Community Development Office. But you just missed them." She glanced over at the clock on the wall. "They closed an hour ago."

"Closed?" *We came all this way for nothing?*

Gina fought back a smile. *Told ya.*

"I'm afraid so," the town clerk replied. She saw his shoulders droop and the look of defeat on his face. "But..." she added with a smile.

Gina held her breath. *No...no...don't say it...*

"I have something in the vault that might help you."

She disappeared around the corner and came back a few seconds later carrying a large bound volume that she slid onto the counter.

Gina wilted into a chair near the door. *We were so close to being done with this...*

"What building are you interested in?"

"The old courthouse," Nathan said.

"Ahh...the courthouse. That's an interesting building. And what was it you wanted to know?"

"Who built it," Nathan replied.

"Right...who built it," she said slowly. "The Registry of Deeds has that information..."

Gina immediately stood up. *We're out of here.*

"But I bet we have something that might tell us that."

Gina plopped down in the chair again. *I don't believe this...*

"First we have to find the year it was built." She walked over to a shelf on the wall and removed one of the hardcover books. "That information will be listed here in the Town History," she said, opening the book. She scanned the Table of Contents briefly and then turned to the correct page.

"Wouldn't that tell the name of the builder, too?" Nathan asked.

"No, not on a building that old...OK, here we go."

She brought the book back to the counter and handed it to Nathan. He saw an old picture of the courthouse and right below it was a single line of type.

Courthouse b.1865

"Built in 1865..." he whispered to himself.

"So now," the town clerk said, "we look in here." She opened the large bound volume and began turning pages.

"What's that?"

"These are old Town Reports. Since the courthouse was a municipal building, it would be listed in the Town Report for the year it was built...in this case 1865."

"You have Town Reports from *1865*?"

"Oh yes," the town clerk replied without looking up. "Here it is."

Nathan's heart began to race. *This is it.*

"Let's see now," she said, scanning the page.

Nathan looked over at Gina, who was busy reading one of the brochures. "Hey," he said in a hushed voice. She looked up and saw him waving her over towards the counter.

Come here and see!

"Hmm...that's odd," the town clerk said.

"What?" Nathan asked, turning back to see what she had found.

"I could've sworn the builder was an American, but it looks like I was wrong."

"You found the name?" The excitement was evident in his voice.

Gina put the brochure back in the display and stepped up to the counter.

"It's right here," the town clerk replied. "All monies for the project were paid to a man named...Vasari."

"Vasari?" Gina said. "That sounds Italian."

"That would be my guess," the town clerk replied.

Nathan felt his heart sink. Then he remembered what Ken Owens had told them in the hardware store.

Something with a V.

"Are you sure?" he asked. There had to be something else, some other connection.

"Positive," the town clerk said.

"May I see that?" Gina asked.

"Certainly." The town clerk turned the bound volume around on the counter so Gina could read it. She examined the photo and the supporting information that continued onto the following page. Nathan just stood there dumbfounded.

It doesn't make any sense.

This time was even worse than before.

The diagram in the book...

And he knew it had to be some kind of mistake.

I saw it change color.

Something was missing—it was the only reasonable explanation.

When Gina was done looking at the book, she slid it back across the counter. "Well, that's that," she said brightly, turning towards Nathan, who stood there in a fog, unable to speak.

Nothing. His heart sunk.

"Is there anything else?" the town clerk asked.

"No, but thank you anyway," Gina replied. "That's exactly what we were looking for."

Nothing. Her heart leapt.

She moved towards the door, fighting the temptation to pump her fists in a victory display, but just leaving the Town Hall and riding home would be celebration enough.

"Well if I can be of any further help, feel free to come back," the town clerk said.

Gina nodded politely, hiding her true feelings. *Don't count on it.*

They walked back outside in complete silence. Nathan's head was hung in defeat and the vacant look in his eyes convinced Gina not to push the issue. She was right. He was wrong.

Once again.

There was no need to rub his nose in it.

But the look on his face had nothing to do with Raven or the courthouse. Something else was bothering him. It was that name—Vasari. He'd seen it somewhere before, he was sure of it, but where? It took him the entire ride home to unearth it from his memory. But he wasn't sure what it meant, if anything at all. Like everything else in this Alastair Raven mystery, nothing was connected. He had a few bits and pieces, but no way to put them together. It was like a puzzle without a box to show what the end result would look like.

"So you're going to put that book back in the attic now, right?" Gina said as they arrived at Nathan's driveway, which separated their houses.

"Yeah," he said, kicking at a pebble on the sidewalk. He watched it skitter across the driveway and disappear in the grass.

"Hey, don't feel so bad," she said, "we tried...right?"

"I suppose."

"I'll see you tomorrow, OK?"

"Yeah...see you later."

He put his bike away and went straight to his room. The book was right where he left it, on the bedside table. It wasn't vibrating, there were no pages turning or fiery images blasting light into the room—there was nothing. Even if there was, it wouldn't matter.

All that work...nothing but a dead end...

There was one more thing he wanted to check, then he'd take the book back up to the attic and hide it in that old wooden trunk, or leave it on the floor where he found it. Anywhere, as long as he could get in and out of that dreadful room as quick as possible. He picked up the book and took it over to his bed. This time he didn't open to the chapter on Alastair Raven.

He went no further than the Introduction.

Gina went straight to the front hallway and got a pencil and spiral notepad from her backpack. Homework could wait. It was time to celebrate her expert handling of the Town Hall trip, and what better way to do that than relaxing on the couch, playing her favorite word game.

When it came to puzzles, word games and brainteasers, she was the champ. Her teachers knew it...her friends knew it...and her parents knew it, although they gave up buying her puzzle books long ago. They simply couldn't get them fast enough—she was that good.

This particular word game was one of the most challenging. She found it two years earlier in a giant book of puzzles, and it immediately became her favorite. It started with a word. Any word. The idea was to see how many *other* words she could make by rearranging some or all of the letters. Any word was fair game as long as it was a real word.

With pencil and notepad in hand, she went into the living room and curled up on the couch. After careful consideration, she came up with the perfect 'starting word' and the challenge was underway. Ten minutes later she had filled an entire page with words of every size.

Halfway down the second page she stopped writing.

"Wait...a...minute..."

She stared at the page, her eyes wide.

"I don't believe it."

That's when the pencil fell out of her hand.

Nathan read the Introduction, which was an explanation of style in architecture. It was extremely boring, but he read it anyway, paying close attention to the various names and dates. He hadn't gone very far when he found the section he was looking for, the same one he'd skipped over previously, never once thinking he'd ever read it again.

According to the author, the discussion of architectural style could be traced as far back as the 16th century to a man named Giorgio Vasari. *There...*

His pulse quickened as he read more. Giorgio Vasari was a painter, art historian and...architect. When he saw the word he stopped reading and let the book drop in his lap.

Architect.

Finally...a link.

The word hung in his mind as he stared mindlessly at the open pages. Downstairs, he heard the front door open and slam shut. Then the sound of someone running up the stairs. He was just getting up to see who it was when Gina appeared in the doorway; her face was beet red and she was holding her side with one hand.

"You...won't..." she tried to say between gulps of air.

"Is everything OK?" he asked, setting the book aside.

"...Just need to...catch my breath."

"What's wrong?"

"You won't... believe it," she managed to say.

"Won't believe what?"

"It's him," she said. "It's really him."

Chapter Six

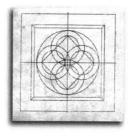

Gargoyles

"What did you say?" Nathan asked. He had a disbelieving look on his face, like he had just swallowed a bug.

Gina hobbled over to the desk and plopped down in the chair. Her hair was in a tangle, and it looked like she crawled through a patch of rose bushes to get there. "After I got home I started playing that game," she said all in one breath.

"Huh?"

"You know, the word game I play all the time?" she said impatiently, waiting for him to catch up. She waved the notepad in the air to jog his memory.

"Oh right," he said with a snort. *Sherlock the English teacher.*

"Wait," she said, opening it on the desk. He shrugged and walked over to the desk to see what had her all worked up. She wasn't one to get easily excited, but now she was talking a mile a minute.

"A lists of words?" he asked sarcastically. *That's what this is all about?*

"That's right." She flipped back to the first page. "And they all came from *this…*"

Nathan's eyes went wide.

Vasari.

But there was more—Gina had used his first name, too. Arlante. She wrote it big, in all caps.

ARLANTE VASARI.

Nathan slapped his hand on his forehead.

AV

"The initials on the courthouse…"

They made perfect sense now. He never bothered to ask for the builder's full name at the Town Hall because he was hoping to hear a different name. When the town clerk said Vasari, he let it go. But Gina, on the other hand, looked at the Town Report. She saw the name. Remembered it.

"Wait…there's more." She moved her finger down to the next line. "I always make small words first."

Nathan looked at the column of words, where she had used random letters from the name to make new words. Simple enough.

Are… aren't…art…

He studied the pattern as she continued explaining. "Then I change the first letter to form even more words."

Vase…vent…veil…vial…

"After the short words, I try to make longer ones." She flipped the page so he could follow her progression.

Rent…rail…rave…

Then he saw where she had stopped. The letters were erratic, as if drawn by a nervous hand.

Raven

"WAIT." He grabbed the notepad and stared at the name. Then he looked at the next line, where Gina had used each of the remaining letters to form *another* word.

Alastair

His jaw dropped open and he stared at Gina, thunderstruck. "This is..." he started to say.

"Spooky, right?" Her eyes were filled with amazement.

He was having trouble finding the right words. Slowly, he shuffled over to his bed and sat down. Only then was he able to put his thoughts in order. "When I found the book...in the basement," he began, never taking his eyes from the notepad. "I knew it was...it had to be...some kind of..." His words were coming out in broken bits and Gina just let him ramble as he connected the dots.

"But this..." he said, staring at the name on the notepad. "It's like a secret code."

"Exactly! And we cracked it. We win!"

"Huh?"

"We broke the code. We solved the mystery."

"What are you talking about?"

"You wanted to know why the book was doing all those weird things. Well now you know." She stood up, satisfied that her work here was done, and sashayed over to the bed.

The Puzzle Champ wins again...trophy please.

She reached out for the notepad but he didn't notice; he was still staring at it, shaking his head back and forth slowly.

"What?" she asked impatiently.

He began to ramble again.

"That *can't* be all there is...there's more...I can feel it..." He looked up at her with a look of utter certainty, his mind made up. "There are too many weird things going on. This is

NOT all of it. There's something else we're supposed to find."

"Oh please," she said, rolling her eyes. "We figured it out. I mean, *I* figured it out. We're done here. Give me the notepad. You're talking crazy-talk."

"No, it's not crazy," he said, "there's something I never told you about Raven."

"Oh boy, here we go," she mumbled under her breath. She folded her arms in protest. *Classic Nathan.*

"He was like...a celebrity...a *really* famous architect."

"Yeah? So?"

"And he disappeared."

"What do you mean?"

"I mean in 1862 he vanished...forever."

Gina considered that for a moment, staring blindly at the far wall, then down at the notepad, then at Nathan's solemn face.

"But he *didn't* vanish," Nathan continued. "Just his name. We know that now, thanks to you. We also know that the courthouse was built in 1865. That was 3 years *after* he disappeared."

"Exactly," Gina said.

"What's that supposed to mean?"

"It's simple. He wanted you to know his secret. That's all. I have no idea why, but it explains why the book was on the table in the basement, next to the calendar. He wanted you to find the photo of the hardware store, which would take you downtown...right past the courthouse. It all makes perfect sense now."

"No, I don't agree," he said, shaking his head defiantly.

"Why not?" Her voice was getting louder by the minute. *He's doing it again.*

"Because what if…" he began.

"STOP," she said, holding up her hand like a crossing guard. "Don't even start."

"But…"

"No. A good mystery is one thing, but now you're taking it too far. And you know what happens every time you do that."

"I have no idea what you're talking about," he said, folding his arms across his chest.

"Really? I guess you forgot about the tree fort."

He scowled and looked away. The tree fort had resulted in a broken leg—his.

"Or how about… your giant sling shot?" she asked.

This time he rolled his eyes. That was how he dented the side of his father's brand new car.

"There was the double tire swing…and let's see…oh yeah…the snow tunnel?"

Nathan covered his mouth with his hand so she couldn't see him biting his lip.

"Then there was the blender experiment…*and*…let's not forget your '*amazing*' washing machine trick." She put extra emphasis on the word amazing.

"OK…OK…I get the point," he said, stopping her before she could get to the rest of his failed ideas.

"Look…" she said, "you were right." Her tone was softer now. "The book led you to the truth. This guy, Raven, wasn't dead after all. He built something without anyone knowing it. But that's all it is. You found a buried treasure, an undiscovered gem, whatever you want to call it. Just be happy with that."

"Well I'm not." He closed the notepad. "I think there's more to this, and I'm going to find out what it is."

She exhaled loudly. "Have it your way." She reached out and snatched the notepad from his hand. "But you're wasting your time."

She left the room without another word and he sat on the edge of his bed thinking.

She's wrong.

He was filled with a new energy.

I have proof now...

He reached over and picked up Compton's Journal.

And I have this.

It brought him this far.

That's all I need.

It would take him the rest of the way.

With book in hand, he sat cross legged on his bed and read the chapter on Alastair Raven for the third time. It was another first in the life of Nathan Cole, but that thought never once entered his mind—he was too busy poring over every word on the page.

There has to be something here.

Scrutinizing every picture.

A clue that I overlooked.

Committing everything to memory.

Some important detail.

"Well now that's a sight to see...my son with a book."

The voice startled him, and he looked up to see his mother standing in the hallway. "Oh...hi Mom." He quickly closed the book, using the tip of his finger as a bookmark.

"What's that you're reading?"

"Uh...just homework," he said, big test tomorrow."

"Really...what subject?" She moved from the hall into his doorway.

"History," he replied in a grim voice, like it was something brand new that she wouldn't understand. *So you don't need to...*

"History?" Her face lit up and she marched into the room.

Nathan moved his right arm over the book to shield it from view. "Yeah, I've got a *ton* to read before..."

"I love history," she said, cutting him off. "It was my favorite subject." There was no stopping her now, and Nathan's heart was racing as she came walking over to the bed.

"Probably got it from my father. He was quite the history buff, you know."

Nathan was too petrified to speak and could only nod.

Isn't that nice.

"Anyway," she said, reaching down to tousle his hair, "I came to tell you—it's time to get washed up for dinner."

That night, his dreams were haunted by a recurring image from the book—a gargoyle with piercing eyes and a jagged mouth that snarled at him with long curved fangs. A massive pair of ribbed wings loomed high over its shoulders, and its enormous claws were open and flexing.

Time and time again it emerged from the swirling gray mist, and each time he circled away. Finally, when he turned to run, the gruesome creature charged him, grabbing him with its massive claws. He struggled desperately to break free, but the gargoyle was much too powerful. As its razor sharp claws tore at his shoulder he bolted from his sleep.

He awoke in a cold sweat, his body shaking with fear as one startling image burned in his memory. It was that horrifying moment when he felt his arm being torn off.

When he did finally open his eyes, he pushed the thought away, deep into that dark place where disquieting dreams go when the night is done. He heard the gentle sound of rain pelting his window and rolled over to check the time on his alarm clock.

WHAT?

He threw back the covers and vaulted out of bed.

Why didn't my alarm go off?

As he stumbled across the room to the bureau, he noticed the book propped open on his desk. It had been on his bed when he fell asleep, and it being on the desk now could only mean one thing. He hurried over at once and searched the open pages.

What do you want to show me?

In the lower right corner, he saw a diagram that he recognized immediately, and for several seconds it held his attention. It was a gargoyle—the same creature from his dream—although this one had a round, almost child-like face. There were no dark eyes, crooked fangs, or menacing wings. As he studied its delicate features it slowly faded away. One second it was there, the next it was gone.

Whoa...

His felt a surge of nervous energy as he stood staring at the blank square in the text. It looked like the printer had mistakenly left something off the page.

"Nathan?" his mother called from down the hall. He looked over at the clock and grimaced, and when he turned back to the book the image had returned.

Huh?

"NATHAN?"

He turned and yelled, "YEAH...I'M COMING."

The book would have to wait. He got dressed in record time and raced downstairs. By the time he got outside, the door to the bus was just closing, and he made a mad dash across the lawn.

"WAIT!"

He reached the bus just as it was pulling away from the curb, and he had to pound on the door to get the driver to stop.

"That was close," Gina said with a chuckle, as he sat down next to her.

"Hey," he said, slightly out of breath. His mind was abuzz with the events in his room, which were amplified by the adrenaline pumping through his body.

"We have our presentation today," she reminded him. *Which I assume you forgot about.*

"Yeah." *A gargoyle image that disappears and then reappears?*

"Do you want to go first or should I?" *No wait, let me guess.*

"OK." *The morning after...that dream....*

"Well, which is it?" She looked over at him waiting for an answer, but he never met her gaze; he just stared straight ahead with a blank expression.

"Whatever." *That can't be a coincidence.*

"Fine," she huffed. *I knew it.*

They rode the rest of the way in silence. She knew full well why he was being so short—he was still mad about their conversation in his room. And all she did was tell him the truth. If he was going to hold a grudge about that, then so be it. She could care less.

I found the missing link.
I solved the mystery.
Let it go, Nathan.

Throughout the day, Nathan's mood never changed. Every time Gina tried to start a conversation with him, he'd respond

97

with little more than a grunt or a one-word answer. When it came time for their presentation, she did all the talking. There was no way she was going to let him ruin all her hard work.

"This red line...(pointing)...shows the Appalachian Trail. It's over 2,000 miles long and goes through 14 states."

Nathan stood next to her trying to look interested, but thoughts and images were looping through his mind like a runaway slide show.

Darkness...gargoyle...fangs...

Gina glared at him, then cleared her throat. "This *blue* line right here is the Continental Divide Trail. The section that goes through the United States is over *3,000* miles long and goes through *five* states."

Her words barely registered in his mind as the images got darker and darker.

Running...trapped...claws...NO!

She spoke louder, but still he remained lost in another world. "And this green line is the Pacific Crest Trail. It goes through three states, from the Canadian border to the Mexican border. That's over 2,600 miles."

The sound of the class applauding finally jolted Nathan out of his dark stupor. As he meandered back to his seat, the gargoyle images flickered briefly and then faded away. But the disturbing images from his dream and the vanishing image from the book were connected by the same common thread. And that told him exactly what he needed to do next.

Gina sat down, confident that she had scored them at least a B+ with her interesting facts and precise artwork. But it could have been so much better.

If only Nathan had made an effort...

"That was great," her friend Amanda whispered.

"Thanks," Gina said with a half-hearted smile.

"Next up," the teacher announced, "Vanessa Duncan and Danny Beecher with their presentation on ancient Egypt."

"Beecher creature," Amanda hissed softly. "They're made for each other."

Gina nodded...*definitely*...as Vanessa Duncan strutted to the front of the room carrying a large shopping bag in both hands.

"Hey, what's up with him?" Amanda whispered, nodding in Nathan's direction.

Gina looked over and saw Nathan staring absentmindedly out the window.

"Who knows?" she said with a shrug, keeping the truth to herself. She could hardly contain her anger.

He's obsessed with a dead man...

But the part that bothered her the most was that he wouldn't listen to her anymore. She closed her eyes and gritted her teeth.

LET IT GO!

She turned her attention to the front of the class where Vanessa was busy pulling various relics out of the shopping bag and arranging them on the chalk tray. The classroom door opened and Danny Beecher made a dramatic entrance dressed as King Tut, which drew an immediate response from the class.

Most of the students laughed. Some hooted. A few others cheered. Nathan never took his eyes from the window. He was busy concocting a plan.

As soon as he got home, Nathan dumped his backpack in the front hall and made a beeline for the garage. He climbed on his bike and rode downtown, never once second guessing his decision to go. It all made sense now.

A gargoyle dream...
A gargoyle image in the book...
In a chapter about Alastair Raven...
Haunted by Alastair Raven...
Who secretly built the courthouse.

When he arrived at the courthouse, he promptly left his bike on the sidewalk and started up the stone steps, scanning the building from top to bottom in search of the next piece in the puzzle.

You're here, I know you are...

Something overhead caught his eye and he stopped.

Hold on...

On each corner of the building, just below the roof line, was a curious outcropping that sloped outward towards the street. They were clearly part of the original structure and had fallen prey to an invasion of thin leafy vines, which covered them like a shiny green blanket.

He blinked hard several times trying to understand what they were, then continued up the steps for a closer inspection.

Why didn't I see those before?

That's when he noticed a thin stream of water leaking from the end of each one—the last of the morning's rain.

"Ahh...rainspouts."

Then he remembered something he read.

Wait a minute...

It was in Compton's Journal.

The year 1200...

It all came back to him.

Rainwater...

He ran back down to the sidewalk and rounded the side of the massive steps to a small plot of withered grass that

100

comprised the front corner of the property. When he looked up, the rainspout was overhead. That's when he saw them. Through the sheath of vines, the shape and the symmetry was undeniable.

Wings.

They fanned outward from each side of the rainspout that was turned down at a slight angle towards the ground. Water dripped from the jagged opening, through a set of spiked incisors.

Fangs.

His legs gave out and he stumbled backwards onto the sidewalk. With his heart pounding he squinted at the swirling gray cloud cover overhead and saw his nightmare come to life all over again.

"Gargoyle."

Chapter 7

The Tempest

He stumbled wildly through the dark. Both of his arms were fully extended, feeling every inch of the darkness in hopes of touching a wall, a door—anything familiar. There was nothing but a damp mist that chilled his face and raised the hairs on the back of his neck. How long had he been walking? There was no way to tell. And why wasn't anyone answering his calls for help?

A muffled sound from close by stopped him in his tracks. Was it behind him? To the side?

"WHO'S THERE?"

A heavy flutter of wings was his only answer, followed by husky breathing, throaty and wet. Fear gripped him and he exploded into a desperate run, using every bit of energy he could muster. But moments later, over his own labored breathing, he heard the sound of wings once more, matching him step for step.

He was quickly losing ground and his legs were burning with fatigue. Then, out of nowhere, a searing pain tore through his shoulder as a massive claw dug into his skin with a vice-like grip and pulled him down.

"HEY."

The nightmare slowly dissolved as the muddy images lost definition and fell away. At the same time, he became aware of someone clutching his shoulder and shaking him. They were calling to him in a faraway voice.

"Wake up."

With unsteady hands, he rubbed his eyes and began to breath normally again.

It was only a dream...only a dream...

"Are you OK?"

He recognized Gina's voice...then the familiar creaks and groans of the school bus...and with it the clamor of kids voices. "Yeah." He pulled himself up in the seat, blinking hard several times as his eyes slowly adjusted to the light.

Gina saw his tired eyes and dazed look. She creased her brow. Why did he look so exhausted at this time of day? "You were having quite the dream."

"Why do you say that?" He grimaced as he rubbed the sore muscles in the back of his neck.

"Your whole body was twitching. It was like...I don't know...you were having a seizure or something."

He gave a slight nod and exhaled.

If you only knew.

She tilted her head. "What did you do, stay up all night reading that dumb book again?"

He should have responded to the snub, but he didn't have the energy. "Not exactly." Then he half turned towards her. "But...wait...where were *you?*"

104

"I was back there," she said, pointing over her shoulder. "You don't remember seeing me when you got on the bus...late...AGAIN?"

"Uh...not that I recall." He turned and stared out the window, trying to remember even *getting* on the bus. Everything from the last two days was mashed together into one shapeless blur obscured by his recurring nightmare.

"I thought you were sitting there reading," she quipped.

"I wish I was," he replied. never taking his eyes from the window.

Anything to keep that nightmare from coming back.

She did a double take.

I wish I was? Since when?

For several long seconds, she watched him as he stared mindlessly out the window, his face void of expression, like it was made of plaster. But his eyes were the creepiest of all—vacant and unmoving—watching the storefronts roll past the window but seeing none of them. Something was going on in that wacky brain of his, and she immediately became suspicious.

The bus came to a squeaking stop in front of the school. Nathan climbed to his feet, still tight from being twisted up like a pretzel. The last remaining fragments of his dream were safely tucked away now, and as he hobbled up the aisle he turned his thoughts to the courthouse. The startling discovery of the gargoyle rainspout confirmed what he felt ever since Gina learned the true identity of Arlante Vasari.

There's more to this.

And it told him something else.

It's inside the building.

"You doing anything this weekend?" Gina asked as they stepped down off the bus.

105

"Huh?" Her question broke his train of thought and he stumbled off the last step.

"This weekend," she repeated, trying not to laugh as he regained his balance, "what are you *doing?*" She was tempted to slap him behind the head and yell...*PAY ATTENTION!*...but he was having enough trouble walking as it was.

"Uh...nothing..." Somehow he had to get inside the courthouse.

"Do you want to work on our life sciences homework together?"

He didn't answer. *But what am I walking into?*

"You do remember it's due on Monday, right?"

Still no reply. *Is it dangerous?*

She stopped walking and demanded, "Are you even listening to me?"

He took three more steps before he realized she wasn't walking beside him anymore. When he finally stopped and turned around, she was standing there glaring at him. "Just as I thought," she snorted as she brushed past him and stormed inside the school.

She managed to cool down by the end of art class. On her way through the crowded hallway, she spied Nathan standing alone at his locker.

Ladies and gentlemen...Round 2.

He was taking a book out of his backpack and putting it on the top shelf when she popped in next to him. "Hey there."

He looked over briefly. "Oh...hi."

OK, she thought to herself, *if he won't talk on his own...I'll MAKE him talk.*

106

"Want to see what I made in art?" Before he could answer, she opened her notebook and pulled out a sheet of heavy paper layered with strips of colored tissue paper. The image was a pastel sunset in red and orange over a peaceful lake in shades of blue and purple, inspired by a photo she saw in the calendar. But she kept that detail to herself.

No need to bring that up again.

Another quick glance. "Very nice." Then he turned back to his locker again, trying to remember what book he needed.

"Want to know how I did it?"

He continued to stare into his locker without answering.

"I can show you after school."

"Uh...no thanks.

What's with all the questions?

"What are you doing during study hall?"

He slammed his locker shut. "Not sure." Then he pushed past her and joined the drove of students trudging down the hallway to their next classes.

"Hey wait..." she blurted out, but he was lost in the sea of bodies and well out of sight. She tucked the collage back in her notebook, taking great care not to wrinkle it, even though part of her wanted to crumple it up and throw it at him. He was SO up to something and it was really starting to make her mad.

He avoids me...

Won't talk to me...

He doesn't listen...

It's like he's under some kind of spell...

Then it dawned on her.

Oh no...not that.

107

After lunch, when it came time for study hall, Nathan got permission from the teacher to go to the library—the one place where Gina wouldn't think to look for him. After her display at his locker, he was on full alert.

I know what she wants...

He'd seen this sneaky side of her before. Gina, the modern day Sherlock Holmes.

She wants to know what I'm up to.

And if she knew what he was planning, she would stop at nothing to get him to quit. He was wandering aimlessly down one of the aisles when a book title caught his eye.

Gothic Architecture and Stone Cutting, An Illustrated Guide.

He quickly pulled it off the shelf, and when he saw the menacing face of a gargoyle on the cover he flinched and dropped the book on the floor.

"MISTER COLE!"

The stern voice came from the end of the aisle, where Mrs. Pierce, the school librarian, was standing with a small mountain of books in one hand. "Is that the way we treat books?"

"Uh...no...sorry," he said. "It just slipped."

She pursed her lips and shot him a skeptical look over the tops of her half-moon glasses.

Is that so?

He quickly picked up the book and hurried in the opposite direction, over to one of the tables in the corner where no one would bother him. Sitting with his back to the rest of the room, he turned back the front cover and quickly became engrossed in the photos and illustrations, many of which he'd seen before and could name without a second's delay.

When he came to the section on gargoyles, he pulled back momentarily. Staring up at him was not just any gargoyle, but the same gargoyle from his dream. He stared in horror at the piercing eyes and gaping jaw, set with long spiked fangs. It was crouched down, with its claws open, poised to attack. His skin tingled as he recalled the damp air gripping him like a giant hand, and he quickly turned the page.

The chapter that followed discussed another type of ornamental decoration called chimeras. Like gargoyles, chimeras were decorative additions to buildings, although they weren't used as waterspouts. They could be imaginary or even grotesque-looking beasts. He was reading about them when a voice broke the silence.

"So this is where you disappeared to."

He turned and saw Gina standing directly behind him.

So much for my library idea.

"What's this?" she asked, leaning over his shoulder for a better look. "Picking out your Halloween costume?" She took one look at the picture and felt a twinge of dread. Whatever that thing was, it was creepy.

Just like that Raven guy.

"They're called chimeras."

"How nice," she said, like she'd just eaten a slug.

He knew there was another one of her annoying questions coming, so he slammed the book shut. "Yeah," he said abruptly as he got up from the table, "they're pretty cool." Before she could respond, he moved past her and disappeared into the maze of bookshelves.

Undaunted, she sat down at the table and waited for him to return.

This is perfect.

She desperately needed to talk to him.

It's totally quiet.

Find out what he was up to.

He won't make a scene.

Hoping very much that she was mistaken.

She waited for several minutes, and when he didn't return she got up and walked around the entire room, casually checked every aisle and table. Before long it became apparent that she was wasting her time—he was nowhere in sight.

"He did it *again*," she snarled as she walked towards the door.

"Gina? Is there a problem?"

The voice surprised her, and she quickly turned and saw Mrs. Pierce standing behind the main desk.

"Oh...no...no problem. I was just looking for someone," she explained as calmly as possible.

Nathan Cole is the problem, she thought to herself.

Then she noticed a book sitting on the counter. It had a gruesome winged creature on the cover with evil eyes and long curved fangs. She walked over at once and opened it up, then began hastily flipping through the pages. When she came to the photo of the chimera she froze.

"Are you interested in Gothic architecture?" Mrs. Pierce asked. "We have several more excellent books on the subject. I'd be happy to show them to you."

"Uh...no...thanks," Gina said as she closed the book and slowly backed away from the counter, unable to take her eyes from the cover. The realization coursed through her body like an electric current.

He never put the book back in the attic.

She wobbled as she turned and walked towards the door.

He's still obsessed with it.

Her worst fears had just been confirmed.

He's not going to stop.

After Nathan left the library he did his best to avoid her altogether. Their encounter on the bus, in the hallway, and in the library, made it clear that she wasn't going to leave him alone. In language arts class, he sat in the back corner of the room, as far from her as he could. She looked his way several times, but he pretended to be paying attention and taking detailed notes, all the while thinking about the courthouse and how he was going to get inside. His choices weren't very promising. As he sat in his chair, with his elbow on the desk and his chin in his hand, he listed each option in his notebook, evaluating them one at a time.

Front door.

He thought about that for a moment and then crossed it off; it was sure to be locked and he couldn't force it open.

Window.

 Maybe, but where? There were none on the ground level, and with a ladder he'd never reach one on the upper floors. He crossed that off, too.

Vent.

That was an interesting option. He'd seen vents on buildings before, even big ones down near the ground. But weren't they usually...?

"Still with us, Mr. Cole?"

He looked up and saw Mr. Tremblay standing at the front of the room with a small hardcover book propped open in his hand.

"Uh...yeah," he said, quickly closing his notebook.

"Excellent. So what do you think he's feeling?"

He felt the eyes of the entire class on him. "Feeling?"

Mr. Tremblay glanced at the book and read aloud in a booming voice. "The tempest in my mind doth from my senses take all feeling else...save what beats there."

111

The classroom was deathly quiet as he looked back at Nathan. "What does that passage tell us about the character's feelings?"

Nathan gulped. Several seconds passed but they felt like minutes. Nothing was coming to mind.

"OK," Mr. Tremblay said, breaking the silence, "let's try it this way. I'll read a portion of the passage, and you tell me what you think the author is trying to convey." He read again, but this time only the first part. Without the drama. "The tempest in my mind…"

Nathan concentrated for a moment and then, "Uh…he has something on his mind?"

"Yes he does," Mr. Tremblay replied, hope evident in his tone. He read on. "Doth from my senses take all feeling else…"

Nathan slumped his shoulders and exhaled.

Why couldn't people just talk normal back then?

"Mr. Cole?"

"Um…takes…something…from his senses?"

"Close enough. And finally, 'save what beats there'…"

"Except for…the thing…he's feeling?"

"That's correct," Mr. Tremblay beamed, "which is…?"

"The tempest?" *Whatever that is.*

"Exactly. What the character is saying here is that this tempest, this *storm* in his mind…"

"It's all he thinks about," Nathan blurted out.

"Yes, that's exactly…"

"And he can't think about anything else but that one thing."

"Bravo, Mr. Cole." He closed the book and glanced up at the clock. "We're just about out of time, so let's stop here.

Just a reminder...tomorrow is Friday, and you know what that means."

The class let out a collective groan. Everyone except for Nathan, who was busy contemplating the tempest in his own mind—a storm that haunted him, challenged him, and on more than one occasion scared the wits out of him.

I need to get past it.

It was time to find whatever Raven wanted him to find.

Put the storm to rest.

Only then would his life return to normal.

Stop the nightmares.

But to make that happen, he had to get ready.

He was just packing up his things as the bell rang to end the class. When he finally walked out of the room, Gina was waiting for him in the hallway.

"We need to talk," she said, stepping directly into his path.

He stopped short to avoid bowling her over. "Whoa...about what?"

"YOU," she shot back.

"Me." It wasn't a question.

"Yeah...what are you doing?" she demanded more than asked.

"I'm standing here talking to you." At the far end of the corridor he saw Mr. Somers, the assistant principal, talking to a group of kids.

"Don't give me that. You know exactly what I'm talking about."

"Actually, I don't." He saw Mr. Somers turn and look at them.

She shook her head in anger as she paced back and forth. "Ohh...I should have known. This is why you've been acting so *strange* lately."

"I have no idea what you're talking about." Mr. Somers craned his neck to see who was making the noise.

She stomped her foot. "YES you DO. You've been purposefully avoiding me."

"I have?"

The group of kids dispersed, and Mr. Somers started walking briskly towards them. He was two classrooms away and Nathan knew it was only a matter of seconds before he'd reach them.

She stabbed at him angrily with her finger. "DON'T deny it...you're hiding something from me."

"Hiding something? Why would you think that?" One classroom away and closing fast.

She turned and kicked a locker. "How come you keep ditching me?"

"I'm busy." Almost there.

She leaned closer and snarled. "With WHAT?"

"Stuff," he said, watching her face turn a warm shade of red. He waited for the perfect moment and then artfully turned and walked away.

"MISS McDermott!"

The loud voice made her jump, and when she turned around her eyes went wide in shock.

She gulped. "Mr. Somers?"

He just appeared out of nowhere, and the way he looked was completely foreign to her—arms folded and shaking his head in disapproval.

She gritted her teeth.
NATHAN YOU RAT!

"Did I just see you kick that locker?"

She looked down at the floor. "Yes."

"Why don't we go to my office and talk about that."

She slumped her shoulders.

No...this isn't happening.

He had it all wrong.

Nathan Cole is the troublemaker...not me.

"After you," he said in a disappointed tone, gesturing towards the far end of the corridor with his hand.

She'd walked by the principal's office many times but had never gone *in* it. As she marched down the hall, she clenched her fists until they were drained of color.

This isn't over, Nathan Cole. Not by a long shot!

Chapter 8

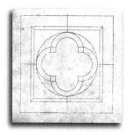

Preparations

"UNBELIEVABLE," Gina fumed as she paced back and forth angrily in her bedroom. "He ditched me AGAIN." She grabbed a stuffed animal off her bureau and heaved it across the room. "AND got me in TROUBLE." She snatched another stuffed animal and slammed it on the rug, seething over the grueling 20 minute lecture from Mr. Somers on the 'proper' treatment of school property, and even worse—the resulting detention.

She looked around for something to kick and took out her wrath on the stuffed animal lying on the floor. It rocketed through the air and bounced off the closet door with a soft thud.

"I'll show him," she snarled. She folded her arms and started to pace again. "Thinks he can fool me...I know he's up to something...still obsessed with that stupid book....after he told me he'd..."

Wait a minute.

She stopped pacing.

That's it...the book!

Nathan was digging frantically through his desk drawer looking for his flashlight when a curious thought made him stop and sit up.

Whatever happened to Gina?

The last time he saw her she was walking down the hallway in the opposite direction with Mr. Somers, towards the main office.

"Rule #1," he said, as he resumed his search, "always watch your back."

He found the flashlight under some comic books and flicked it on. Nothing. It went on top of the desk for the time being, until he could find some batteries. Next item on the list, his Swiss Army knife.

What did she mean?... "You're hiding something from me."

Did she know what he was planning?

Impossible...how could she?

He never told her about his visit to the courthouse, or finding the gargoyle rainspouts. Never told her about his recurring dream. Her nonstop questions were just her way of tricking him into revealing what he was doing.

So she can talk me out of it.

All the more reason to avoid her completely until he finished his search of the courthouse. He found his Swiss Army knife in the side drawer and set it next to the flashlight, then went downstairs to find batteries and a few other things on his list.

When he had everything assembled on his desk, plus some other odds and ends he found along the way, he reviewed his plan of action. After school tomorrow he would empty his backpack, then repack it with his collection of tools. Then, early Saturday morning, he would ride downtown and...

And what?

That's where his plan ended. There was still one huge obstacle—how he was going to get inside the building. He grabbed the notebook from his backpack and looked over his list of possible entry points for the umpteenth time. Any one of them could provide the answer, but he wasn't that naive.

None of these are going to work.

Ken Owens said it himself. *"The doors are all locked."*

He gritted his teeth and ripped the page out of the notebook.

I've come too far to stop now.

Crumpled it into a ball.

I have to finish this.

And threw it angrily at the wall.

For several minutes he just sat there stewing. Then it dawned on him.

Wait a minute...

He picked up the crumpled paper and smoothed it out.

This list means nothing.

Two times he had gone to the courthouse, once with Gina and once alone. During both of those visits he was so preoccupied with a specific part of the building that he ignored the rest of it.

Never looked at the side.

His frustration started to fade.

Never checked around back.

Until he examined the whole place, it was impossible to know if he could get inside or not.

It's a huge building.

Maybe there was something he missed.

On Friday morning, Gina sat on the bus with a devious grin on her face.

Yes...I'm brilliant.

She had devised the perfect plan. It was so good that she couldn't believe she hadn't thought of it earlier, but then again, Nathan had never acted like this before—never made her this angry before—never *ever* betrayed her like he had in the hallway.

Now the whole office staff thinks I'm a troublemaker.

That was all the reason she needed to do it.

I'm getting rid of that book...for good.

It had proven nothing but trouble from the start and had turned her friend into a completely different person. His obsession with the book had made him distant at times and outright cold at others.

Oh...speak of the devil.

Nathan appeared at the front of the bus and stood for a moment surveying the seats for an open spot. His hair was uncombed, and he was out of breath from running.

Almost missed the bus…again.

She immediately turned and looked out the window, gritting her teeth as her anger sparked and crackled. She fought back the sudden urge to stick out her leg and trip him as he walked by her seat.

Yeah...that's it...keep walking.

Once he was past her, her crafty smile returned. He had no idea what kind of trouble he had stirred up. First, she'd find the book, which was probably in his bedroom. Where else would he keep it? Once she smuggled it out of his house, she'd simply throw it away in a place where no one would find it. The incinerator in the school basement would be perfect, or maybe downtown in a smelly old restaurant dumpster. Someplace where it would go and never come back. Then things would finally return to normal.

No more book.

No more weird Nathan.

And the winner is...envelope please...GINA McDERMOTT!!

Nathan saw Gina look away and walked quickly down the aisle. The angry look on her face told him everything he needed to know and he tried not to laugh out loud.

Mission accomplished.

If Gina was mad at him, she wouldn't be hounding him about his business anytime soon. No more nagging questions or surprise visits in the library.

He made his way towards the back of the bus and collapsed into an empty seat away from the other kids. The latest gargoyle dream had him tossing and turning through the night and it was a struggle to stay awake. But as the bus chugged up the street, rocking him ever so gently in the seat, his eyelids began to droop and he didn't try to fight it.

Maybe just a short nap.

His eyelids slid shut.

Just for a few minutes.

And the world around him slowly drifted away.

"LOOK AT THAT!"

The shout rocked him out of his slumber. His eyes shot open and he saw the kids at the front of the bus pressed against the right side windows, pointing at one of the small downtown shops. Two police cruisers were parked at the curb and the front door of the shop was roped off with yellow crime scene tape.

"COOL," someone yelled.

The bus stopped for the red light, and Nathan got a clear view of the shattered front door and the sidewalk that sparkled in the morning sun with tiny bits of broken glass. Through the large plate glass window he saw two policemen at the front counter speaking to the owner. The three of them were busy looking at something on top of the counter.

Kelly Giles, a fourth grader that Nathan knew, but rarely spoke to, was sitting across the aisle and looked over with mild interest. "Someone broke in early this morning," she said in a humdrum voice.

"How do you know that?" Nathan asked.

"My dad." She spoke without taking her eyes from the window. "He's a policeman. He told us about it this morning at breakfast."

Nathan gulped. *A break in.* Wasn't that what he was planning to do at the courthouse? Seeing the smashed door, the broken glass and the police cruisers gave him a bad feeling in the pit of his stomach.

"They'll catch the guy who did it," Kelly said very matter-of-fact. Then she looked at Nathan for the first time, her eyes locked on his like she was reading his deepest thoughts and knew exactly what he was planning to do.

He felt a nervous twinge in his chest.

"I bet they already did."

"No way," Nathan balked.

Kelly raised both eyebrows and nodded her head with absolute certainty. *Oh yes they did.*

"How?" Nathan asked in a skeptical tone, as the traffic light changed and the bus roared through the intersection.

"Hidden cameras."

Nathan felt another jab of anxiety. *Cameras?*

"My dad said they recorded the whole thing."

Nathan's eyes went wide. *Recorded?*

"There's even one that shows the front sidewalk," she added, "so whoever broke in, they can see which direction he came from and what he was driving."

Nathan slumped in the seat, staring at the floor.

Does the courthouse have cameras?

The building wasn't in use anymore, but did that even matter?

How else would they keep it secure?

The disturbing image of two policemen escorting him down the steps of the courthouse and into the backseat of a police cruiser flashed in his mind. It jolted his senses like the sudden screech of car tires. The image was still rooted in his mind when the bus pulled up to the curb in front of the school.

I'm not a robber, he thought to himself as he stepped off the bus and trudged up the sidewalk towards the school. The usual morning crowd was lumbering along all around him, talking, laughing and shoving each other, but he barely noticed them.

I'm just going in to look around.

He followed the throng of students through the front doors and into the building.

It's not like I'm going to steal anything.

"Did we sleep late today, Mr. Cole?"

Nathan looked up in time to see Mr. Somers standing in his direct path, just outside the door to the main office. If he hadn't spoken up, Nathan would have walked right into him.

"No, but that would've been nice," he replied, stifling a yawn.

"Well, I'll tell you what," Mr. Somers said lightheartedly, "you have my permission to stay home tomorrow morning and sleep as long as you want."

"Gee, thanks," Nathan said with smile. It wasn't often that he and the assistant principal had a humorous conversation. "I really appreciate that."

"Don't mention it.

Gina was standing further down the hallway talking to Amanda, but they both stopped and watched when Nathan nearly plowed into Mr. Somers.

"I wonder what that was about," Amanda said, as Mr. Somers finished talking to Nathan and headed into the main office.

Gina held her breath, desperately hoping to see Mr. Somers hand Nathan a pink detention slip.

For provoking a fellow student.

But when she saw him laugh, she felt her anger start to sizzle all over again.

Just you wait, she told herself as Nathan walked past them on the opposite side of the hallway, a smug look on his face.

You think this is over.

She still couldn't understand how he simply walked away and she got in trouble.

I can't wait to see the look on your face.

She couldn't help but smile, thinking how their conversation would go when she worked her plan to perfection; how he'd tear the house apart looking for that stupid book, only to come up empty handed. Of course, she'd look dreadfully surprised when he told her—she didn't even have to practice.

What's that? You can't find your book?

And genuinely concerned.

Oh my...that's just AWFUL.
Maybe offer him some hope.
Don't worry, I'm sure it'll turn up sooner or later.
NOT!

Nathan's near collision with Mr. Somers was the jolt he needed to snap him out of his funk.
What am I worrying about?
Chances were very good that he wouldn't get inside the courthouse at all, and he'd end up coming right back home.
There's no way I'm breaking in.
As the day wore on, his feelings of dread steadily diminished.
I'm just going to look at the building...that's all.
And were replaced by a growing sense of anticipation.
Who knows what I'll find?

By the time he rode home on the bus, his anticipation had turned to full blown excitement. Even when the bus passed that same downtown shop, with its newly repaired front door, he didn't waver. He looked carefully and saw the small outside cameras that Kelly Giles told him about, mounted high above the sidewalk at each corner of the storefront. They didn't faze him in the least.

At home he emptied his backpack and then carefully repacked it with the tools that were piled on his desk, all the while telling himself the same thing over and over.
I'm just going to look at the building.
He wasn't going to do anything destructive.
Just a young kid looking at the building.
But if the right opportunity presented itself...
Oh look, someone left this door unlocked.

He would do the right thing.
I wonder if everything is all right inside.
Because he was a responsible citizen.
Maybe I'll just check and make sure.

When he finished with the backpack, there was one last thing to do. He got a clean sheet of paper from his desk and wrote his parents a short note. Since he was planning an early start and wanted to avoid a discussion with his parents about where he was going, a note was the perfect solution. He'd leave it on the kitchen table where they were sure to find it, and it would buy him all the time he needed.

He chose his words carefully, knowing exactly what to write. He left out the part about going to the courthouse.

After going over her plan to steal the book, Gina decided an old pillowcase would be the best thing to use. It wouldn't be as bulky as her backpack, and she could just throw the whole thing away. There were bound to be some in the rag bag that her mother kept in the closet beneath the stairs, and when it was gone no one would miss it.

She got home from school and went straight to the closet. The rag bag was even heavier than the last time, crammed full of old bed sheets, worn out socks and undershirts, grease-stained tablecloths, and several old pillowcases. She grabbed the first one she saw and took it upstairs, where she smoothed it out and folded it into a compact square. Then she slipped it inside her jacket pocket, where it would remain hidden until the time was right. As it turned out, she didn't have to wait that long.

Her chance came much sooner than expected.

Chapter Nine

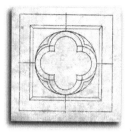

The Courthouse

There was a knock on the bedroom door. Nathan stirred.
Go away.

Seconds later there was another knock, and then he heard his door open. Reluctantly, he pulled back the covers and partially opened one eye, squinting just enough to see the fuzzy outline of someone standing in his doorway.

"Nathan?"

He propped himself up on one elbow and rubbed his eyes. When he opened them again he saw his mother standing there.

"Yeah?"

"Your father and I are going shopping."

"What *time* is it?" he asked, trying to imagine why anyone would go shopping at this hour of the day.

"It's almost eight o'clock."

"Oh…" he replied.

"We have a long shopping list and want to get an early start."

"Whatever," he said as he flopped back down on the bed. His mother closed the door and that's when his eyes shot open in a panic.

EIGHT O'CLOCK?

He threw back the covers and quickly got dressed. By the time he made it downstairs his parents were already gone.

Gina had been up for almost an hour. When she heard the car pull out of the driveway next door, she raced over to the window in time to see it turning the corner at the far end of the street. That's when her adrenaline kicked in.

It's time.

Someone had left Nathan's house, but who was it? His parents? Just one of them? The whole family?

There's only one way to find out.

She pulled on her jacket and patted the pocket to make sure the pillowcase was still there, then she walked out into the hallway. The only sound to be heard was the loud snoring coming from her parents' bedroom. They liked to sleep late on Saturdays and wouldn't be up for at least another hour.

Plenty of time.

She tiptoed down the hallway past their bedroom door, completely unnoticed, and hurried down the stairs.

Nathan swallowed the last bite of a bagel as he slipped out the back door. His bike was leaning up against the side of the house where he left it, and as he rode down the driveway the cool morning air chilled his face. Halfway down the street he thought about going back for his coat but he wanted to get downtown before the street traffic got too heavy. He was late enough as it was.

Gina was just coming out the front door as Nathan reached the end of the block. She never noticed him turning the corner as she made her way across the lawn towards his house. She was too busy practicing what she'd say if he answered the door.

Oh good morning, did I wake you?

That was no good—too phony.

Hello, I know it's early but...

No—too apologetic.

Did I leave my backpack here the other day?

Perfect.

Missing something as important as a backpack was serious, especially if she sounded upset about it. She picked up her pace and when she reached the front porch steps, she paused and took a deep breath.

Here goes.

The front door was solid wood. She pounded on it several times with her closed fist. No answer. She tried again. Still no answer. Her hand was sore, so she turned the knob and gently pushed the door open a few inches.

"Hello?"

There was no response.

"Anybody home?"

The house was completely quiet, so she stepped inside and called again, a little louder this time.

"HELLO...?"

She stood perfectly still, listening for sounds of any kind.

So far so good.

She moved towards the stairs and paused. If Nathan was still asleep, he wouldn't have heard her, especially if his door was closed. She bit the inside of her lip as she looked down the hallway towards the kitchen, then up the stairs to the second floor landing.

Just stick to the plan.

She took a deep breath and started slowly up the stairs.

Nathan came within two blocks of the old courthouse when he saw a large truck parked next to the curb. Two men were unloading wooden barriers from the back of it and setting them on the sidewalk. They paid no attention to him as he rode past. A little farther up the road he saw dump trucks, the same kind he'd seen on his street when they repaved it the previous summer. Standing nearby was a group of men drinking coffee and exchanging jokes. One of them glanced his way briefly, but then shoved his face into a paper wrapper for another bite of his breakfast sandwich.

Nathan crossed the street and rode past the group, using the trucks to block him from view. When he was well past the last truck, he crossed back over and continued down the street. The courthouse was in plain sight.

Dead ahead.

Gina reached the top of the stairway and stopped to listen. There was no sound at all.

"Hello?" Her voice was met by an eerie silence. No one was snoring, watching television or using the shower.

There's no one here.

She felt a sudden wave of guilt at being in someone else's house alone, and she had to keep reminding herself why she was there.

I have to get rid of that book.

She tiptoed down the hallway.

Nathan's my friend.

The door to his room was wide open.

I have to destroy it.

She eased forward and peaked inside.

Before it can do more harm.

His bed was empty and the covers were tossed every which way. Then her eyes locked onto the bedside table.

There it is!

She smiled and eased the pillowcase out of her coat pocket, then stepped into the room.

This is going to be easier than I thought.

Nathan biked to the next block and stopped short. The courthouse was directly across the street on the opposite corner.

Huh?

There was a problem. A utility truck was parked at the curb and two men were standing at the front door. Both were wearing gray zip-up work suits. One of the men was fumbling with the lock while the other man stood nearby looking up at the front of the building.

What are they doing?

He watched as they struggled with the lock. They didn't appear to be in any hurry. Maybe they were just checking something in the building and would leave when they were done. He let out a heavy breath and pulled back out of sight.

It was early yet.

Gina moved slowly across the room towards the bedside table. All she had to do was hold the pillowcase next to it and give the book a quick nudge.

Nice and easy.

But as she neared the table, the book suddenly began to vibrate, making the lamp wobble. She froze in her tracks.

Huh?

She swallowed hard and took a step closer. The book vibrated even harder and the alarm clock started to slide sideways.

She froze again, and everything stopped. A wave of fear rippled through her body as she stood trying to think of what to do next. A full minute passed, the book sitting completely still on the table, and then she decided to try again. But as she lifted her foot off the rug, the book shuddered violently, nearly knocking the lamp over onto the floor. She jumped back, letting out an audible shriek and clutching the pillowcase in her trembling hands.

It's like it knows what I'm doing.

Another icy cold shiver made her body shudder.

I need to find another way to do this.

Very slowly she backed away from the table, never once taking her eyes off the book. She was still backing up when something touched the back of her legs and she let out a muffled scream. When she turned and saw what it was, she let out a long breath.

It's just the desk.

Then she saw the note.

Nathan sat at the corner, watching the activity at the front of the courthouse. The two workmen finally opened the front door and disappeared inside. Seconds later, a second utility truck arrived and two more men got out.

Nathan's heart sank.

No...no...no...

The men glanced up at the front of the building briefly, sipping their coffee, and then climbed the steps and went inside. Nathan decided to stay for a few minutes longer, just to see who they were and what they were doing. His chances of getting inside the building were shrinking by the minute.

Gina recognized Nathan's handwriting at once and picked up the note.

> Mom + Dad,
>   Went to do some research
>   for a school project.
>   Be back later.
>
>   Nathan

It didn't make any sense.
Research?
Since when did Nathan Cole do research?
For a school project?
What school project?
Wait a minute...
She suddenly realized what he was doing.
He didn't go with his parents.
He'd been keeping something from her since Wednesday.
This is it.
The note was just a cover so he could sneak to...
She dropped the pillowcase on the floor and sprinted out of the room. The book would have to wait. Several minutes

later she was on her bike, headed downtown, hoping she wasn't too late.

Nathan got sick of waiting and left the corner. He rode down the sidewalk a short way and stopped. The courthouse was directly across the street, but even from there he couldn't see what was going on inside.

What are they doing in there?

There was no way to know unless he got closer. Much closer. He checked the street in both directions and then looked over at the front door of the courthouse.

All clear.

He bit the edge of his lip.

Maybe just a quick look.

First he needed to stash his bike. He scanned the street in both directions and saw an old alley further up the sidewalk. It was directly across from Owens Hardware.

Perfect.

He rode to the alley and parked his bike a short way in, where he hoped no one would notice it. Then he went back out to street and surveyed the front of the courthouse.

Still clear.

The utility truck gave him an idea, and he scampered quickly up the sidewalk. When he got close enough, he crossed the street and ducked down next to the back tire. From there, the truck provided a perfect shield from the front door.

Just then, the front door of the courthouse opened and one of the workmen came out. Nathan held his breath, hoping he wasn't coming down to move the truck. But as soon as he came through the door, he turned and propped it open, then went back inside.

Nathan's heart raced.

This is it!

He took a deep breath.

Just up to the front door.

And pushed the hair out of his face.

GO!

He jumped out from behind the truck and bolted to the stairs, racing up them two at a time. When he reached the front door, slightly out of breath, he stopped and peeked inside. There were no workmen in sight, just a deserted entryway that lead to the front lobby.

DO IT!

He slipped one foot inside the doorway, then another.

After that there was no turning back.

Gina peddled as fast as she could, blocking out the whirlwind of emotions swirling through her mind. The chill in the air made her eyes water, and she blinked hard to keep them clear. Driveways and mailboxes whizzed past. Soon it was storefronts and side streets. An early morning delivery truck honked and swerved to avoid her as she cut across an intersection. She ignored it and peddled faster.

She was one block from the courthouse when she stopped, her lungs burning as she struggled to catch her breath. The street up ahead was blocked off and there were trucks and men everywhere.

No!

Thinking quickly, she turned and doubled back to a side street she had passed just moments earlier. It would eat up precious time to loop around the block, but it was her only choice—she had to get to the courthouse before Nathan did something dangerous...or stupid.

Again!

A convoy of dump trucks roared past her just as she reached the side street, but she ignored them and sped around the corner. Just then she looked up and saw more roadblocks, and a police cruiser with its blue lights flashing, at the far end of the street. She screeched to a stop, and sat there with her heart racing.

THINK!

Then she saw it—a shortcut—one that would get her past the roadblocks and help her make up the time she already lost. Nathan had gotten a head start and every second was critical if she stood any chance of stopping him. Just thinking his name got her thoughts churning once more.

What is he thinking?

He'd been acting so strange lately.

Did he find another clue?

Treating her like a complete stranger.

That would explain his behavior.

And now he was headed towards something dangerous.

I just know it.

The thought made her ride even faster, bumping over the uneven pavement, past the overflowing trashcans and broken glass that littered the way. She was steering around an overturned garbage can when two dark shapes appeared out of nowhere. Their greasy fur was matted and slick, and at first she thought they were two black cats. Then she saw their long ropey tails. Her scream echoed up and down the alley as she lost control of the bike and swerved into a pile of trash.

Once Nathan was inside the front door he ducked to his left. There was very little light. As he moved through the shadows, staying close to the wall, he could hear men talking somewhere in the distance. Their voices echoed in the darkness and he stayed back for a moment, trying to understand what they were saying.

Gina plowed into a garbage can and went tumbling over the handlebars. Luckily, a pile of cardboard boxes broke her fall. As she climbed out of the heap, she saw something leaning against the building. Her heart raced.

Nathan's bike...

She was right.

He's here!

She quickly climbed to her feet, wiping debris off her clothes and ignoring the smell. There was no time to dislodge her bike, so she just left it there and took off down the alley.

Nathan's vision began to improve as his eyes slowly adjusted to the darkness. He was standing in a small alcove near the entryway, where there would normally be a wall phone or a bench with potted plants. There was neither. Several feet away, through an arched entryway, he saw the main lobby. Just beyond it was the opening to a corridor that was blanketed in darkness. The moment he saw it, he moved out of the shadows and continued on.

That's it.

Gina ran to the end of the alley and stopped just short of the street. She peered over at the courthouse and saw that something was happening. Two trucks were parked in front of the building and the front door was open.

No Nathan. She let out an angry growl and clenched both fists.

He didn't...

Just then she heard a massive roar that echoed between the buildings at the far end of the street, like a giant machine grinding up the city, block by block. It grew louder and louder until finally, a small pickup truck turned onto the street in front of the courthouse. It had a flashing yellow light on its roof and a sign hanging from its bumper that read 'Wide Load.' Right behind it, pitching back and forth from the massive weight, was a giant crane with a huge wrecking ball attached to the boom.

Oh no...

There was no time to lose.

I have to find him.

She ran across the street to Owens Hardware and paused as the crane slowed to make the wide turn around the corner. If she was going to get inside the building, she had to do it before the truck and the crane arrived.

I have to get him out.

By her estimation she had less than thirty seconds.

This is going to be close.

When Nathan reached the entrance to the front lobby, he stopped and peeked around the edge of the doorframe.

I'm inside...I actually made it inside.

A powerful surge of adrenaline made him forget his fear and he stepped into the lobby.

Alastair Raven built this.

Even in the diminished light, he could see that the room was enormous, but unlike other lobbies he'd been in, this one was missing the usual touches. There was no front desk, no waiting area with chairs and tables, and not a single magazine to read. Even more bizarre, there were no lamps or hanging lights anywhere. The walls were stripped bare.

No cameras.

To his immediate left was a stairway that swept up and around to the second level. That's where he heard the men working, moving something heavy across the floor. By the sound of their loud talking and laughing, it was clear they wouldn't be coming downstairs anytime soon.

Gina raced down the sidewalk past the utility trucks. She was so concerned about the crane that she didn't stop when she reached the base of the steps; she sprinted up them and bolted straight through the front door.

There has to be someone working inside.

She'd stop the first person she saw and explain that her friend had wandered inside and could they please help her find him.

Hopefully they'll find him in time.

Nathan heard a loud noise coming from outside on the street, but he ignored it. His full attention was on the dark corridor on the far side of the lobby. Whatever Raven wanted him to see was there—he was sure of it. He took off his backpack and set it on the floor. Just as he was taking out his flashlight, his ears detected another sound.

Footsteps?

Up until now they had been drowned out by the noise of the crane.

Gina darted through the alcove and just kept running. It was dark, but she was so desperate to find someone that she didn't bother to slow down.

139

Nathan was just getting up off the floor when he saw something out of the corner of his eye. He turned to see what it was but he was too late.

Gina saw a shadowy figure rise up directly in front of her. It appeared so abruptly that she couldn't stop or move out of its way. She let out a loud scream as she plowed into it.

Before he could duck out of the way, Nathan was thrown backwards onto the floor. He hit his head on the tile and the flashlight flew out of his hand and went skidding across the floor.

The men upstairs heard the scream and stopped working. As they came running down the hallway, Nathan lay semi-dazed on the floor, trying to see who had knocked him down. With his head pounding in pain, he looked over at Gina, who was holding her head with one hand while trying to push herself off the floor with the other.

"Gina?"

"Nathan?"

"What are you doing here?" he asked.

"I'm saving you," she replied, climbing to her feet slowly.

"Saving *me*?" he asked. "I thought you were done helping me."

"I was…" she said and then stopped. The last thing she wanted to do was admit she'd been snooping around in his bedroom—that she'd found his note. As it was, her head was throbbing so hard that she was having a hard time staying upright.

Nathan heard the men coming and looked over at the flashlight. It was at least ten feet away, right next to a second staircase that led to a lower level. Upstairs, the sound of footsteps was getting louder; the men were just seconds away. He and Gina had to get out of there fast. If they got caught, there was no telling what would happen to them. Visions of being hauled away in a police car filled his head. They were trespassing in a construction zone. Not good.

Get up...get up...

He climbed to his feet, still shaky from his fall, and stumbled over to Gina.

"Come on," he said, taking a hold of her arm, "we have to get out of here."

She started to move, but she was in no better shape than he was. Nathan turned towards the front entryway and stopped short when he saw two men coming up the front steps. They were dressed in the same gray work suits and were wearing bright yellow hard hats.

"We need to find another way out," he said.

Just then, the men on the second level reached the top of the stairs. When they looked down and saw Nathan and Gina standing in the lobby, one of them yelled.

"HEY...STOP!"

After that everything happened very quickly.

Nathan checked the front entrance—the two men in hard hats were coming through the door. He looked up to his right—the workers were starting to come down the stairs. He spun around and looked at the dark corridor—it was close, but he'd need the flashlight to see. There was no way he could get to it and then to the corridor before the men reached them.

There was only one other possibility.

"This way," he said, pulling Gina by the arm.

She was still wobbly, and it took every bit of energy he had to drag her towards the staircase. On the way he bent down and picked up the flashlight, then hobbled down the marble steps, holding Gina with his right hand and the flashlight with his left.

When they reached the bottom of the stairs, he pushed off the banister and punched the button on the flashlight. Nothing happened.

Come on...

He tried it again with the same result.

Are you kidding me?

When he shook it he heard the soft crinkle of broken glass.

Great...a broken bulb.

He jammed it into his backpack as the voices in the main lobby grew louder. One of the men was shouting orders to the others. Any second now they would reach the top of the stairs.

Nathan blocked them out and took Gina's arm, pulling her forward into the heavy darkness. Her head was sore and she had no idea where they were going, but she didn't resist—her desire to get out of the building was as strong as his, although for a very different reason. She had no interest in Alastair Raven, but a lot of interest in the crane outside—Nathan was definitely interested in Alastair Raven, he didn't want to get caught.

She had no idea how long he'd been inside the building, but his quick thinking in the lobby had her convinced that he knew another way out. Maybe it was some back door or emergency staircase. he'd found while he was snooping around. She didn't care...just as long as it got them outside. If she knew that he had entered the building only minutes before she did, she never would have gone down the steps with him. She would have stayed and taken her chances with the workers.

Nathan moved to his left, across the floor to the wall. With any luck they'd find a place to hide where the men couldn't find them, or maybe another stairway up to the first floor. If they could double back somehow, they might be able to sneak out of the building before the men caught up to them. Then it would be a simple footrace.

Kids vs. adults.

He liked his chances.

Once he reached the wall, he felt his way along in the dark using the cold stone surface as a guide. Behind him, at the top of the stairs, the men were yelling at them to return, but he ignored their shouts and kept moving along, pulling Gina with him as he went.

Then he heard footsteps. Their numbers had grown and now the workmen were thundering down the stairs like a herd of hungry animals. Nathan looked back over his shoulder at the stairs, but in the pitch black it was impossible to see. It gave him a momentary feeling of relief.

If we can't see them...they can't see us.

But that could change at any moment.

"Come on, we need to hurry." He spun back around and charged forward when his head collided with something solid and he crumpled to the floor.

Gina gasped. "Nathan?" She knelt down on the ground and searched frantically in the dark until her hand bumped up against him. She shook his body gently. "Nathan...are you OK?"

Behind them, the heavy sound of footsteps on the stairs.

"Nathan! We have to keep moving." She shook him again but he wasn't moving. The men were getting closer.

She shook him harder.

"NATHAN?"

Chapter 10

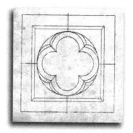

Chimera

"GO GET THE FLASHLIGHT FROM THE TRUCK!"

The voice boomed from the middle of the stairway, where the murky gloom had forced the workers to pause, and it echoed through the darkness of the lower level. It was followed by the frantic sound of footsteps as one of the workers raced back up the stairs to the lobby.

By now, Gina was shaking Nathan repeatedly. "Nathan... get up...get up."

This time he started to move. "Ohh..." he groaned, as he rolled onto his back. A dull pain was pulsating through his skull like the rhythmic toll of a church bell. He reached up to touch his forehead and immediately pulled his hand away.

"What happened?" Gina asked. One minute he was standing right there next to her, and the next he was laid out in a heap on the floor.

"I hit my head..." he said with a grimace, rolling over onto his side.

"On what?"

He propped himself up on one elbow. "I have no idea."

"Can you stand?"

He took a deep breath and leaned on her for support as he struggled to his feet. Once upright, he reached out in the dark to gain his bearings, but his fingers touched nothing but the damp air and he was struck with a terrifying realization.

The dream...

A cold chill shot through his upper body.

Stumbling in the dark...

Dark images from his nightmare burned in his memory.

Trying to get away...

It was all playing out before him in real time.

"We need to find a place to hide," he said with renewed urgency.

"Wait a minute," Gina said, "I thought you knew a way out."

"Not exactly."

"Nathan," she protested, "we need to get out of here."

"Yes, I understand that."

"No, you don't understand." She grabbed his arm. "We need to get OUT of the building." He could hear the genuine fear in her voice. "When I was coming in the front door, there was a crane coming up the street."

"That was probably just..."

"NATHAN!" This time she clamped onto him with both hands, pulling on his arm hard enough to spin him around. The jolt created another sharp streak of pain behind his eyes, and he pressed his hand to his forehead in an attempt to make it stop. "The roads are blocked off in every direction. Men are working in the building. There are dump trucks parked outside. Something major is happening to this building and we have to get out NOW!"

"We can't go back," he said. "They saw us, remember?" He broke free of her grip and backed away. "We've got to...OWW!"

"What is it?"

"My elbow..." He grabbed his left arm that hung weakly by his side and tried to rub away the numbing sensation.

"What now?" she asked.

He clenched his teeth and worked his arm back and forth. "I just hit something."

"Again?"

He reached out with his good arm and swung it tentatively through the air in a wide arc.

There.

His fingertips brushed against something solid.

"What is it?" Gina asked.

"It's a column," he whispered, running his hands over the smooth glassy surface, "made of polished stone." He could picture it in his mind—it was an image that was etched into his memory from hours of reading Compton's Journal. His hands moved higher and higher along the gentle curve of the stone until they grazed another surface. It was a strange carving with bumps and ridges and curious grooves, extending out from the column several inches.

Just then he heard a loud commotion on the stairs. The man who went to get the flashlight had returned and was shining a powerful beam of light back and forth across the stairway. No longer hindered by the darkness, the men quickly proceeded to the lower level.

"You might as well come out," the foreman yelled. "There's nowhere to go."

Nathan grabbed Gina and pulled her back against the wall next to the column as the light swept past them. In that fleeting moment he saw the silhouette of the stone carving on the column. It was half man, half animal, and he recognized the grotesque form at once.

Chimera.

It was the same image he'd seen in the library the day before.

A mythical creature used for decorative purposes.

This one was attached to the column, just above shoulder height. His head still throbbed from walking into it only moments earlier.

"OVER THERE," one of the workmen yelled, and the beam of light swung back to the column. The men were no more than twenty feet away.

"We see you kids," someone yelled. "Come on out."

"...Don't...move..." Nathan whispered, each word spoken in a separate breath. He felt Gina's body trembling and he instantly regretted his decision to come down to the lower level.

The men were fifteen feet away when Nathan's head began to throb even harder. This was going to end badly. Not only would they face the wrath of the workmen, almost certainly the police, and definitely their parents, but the building would be destroyed and whatever Raven wanted him to find would be lost forever.

When the workmen reached ten feet, Nathan felt the strength drain from his legs. Without thinking, he reached up and clutched the side of the chimera to steady himself.

"Listen kids, it's time to stop..."

The workman's voice was cut off when the wall next to the column suddenly gave way and Nathan and Gina were thrown backwards. The workmen heard the sound and rushed forward, shining the light frantically in every direction.

But the only face they saw belonged to the chimera, that taunted them with bulging eyes and flared nostrils. Next to it was nothing but a flat slab of stone where the wall continued down the hallway. The two intruders were gone.

"WHERE DID THEY GO?" the foreman yelled. "THEY WERE RIGHT HERE!" He turned to the man holding the flashlight. "Give me that," he said, ripping it out of the man's hand. "Stupid kids..." he snarled as he checked the wall from top to bottom, inspecting every inch of stone. "They're either magicians, or they know something we don't. People don't just vanish into thin air."

"What now?" one of the workers asked, when it became obvious that they weren't going to find them.

The foreman thrust the flashlight at him and said, "Search the building."

"Huh?"

"SPREAD OUT!" he yelled. "SEARCH THE WHOLE BUILDING." He turned and stormed back up the stairs, shaking his head in disgust and muttering obscenities. The job was already an hour behind schedule, and now this— another hold up. There was no telling how long it would take to find the two kids but at least he had the advantage of manpower. Wherever they were hiding, he'd find them soon enough. It was only a matter of time.

They can't hide forever.

He went up to the first floor and walked outside. The demolition crew was getting ready to set up, and there were a number of things he had to go over with them. By the time he was done, his men would have the two kids in hand. If not...

Too bad.

They were trespassing.

149

Sneaky little brats...
Whatever happened to them was their own fault.

♦

Gina blinked hard and slowly lifted her head. The eerie silence and ink-black surroundings confirmed that they weren't in the downstairs hallway anymore. There was no angry mob or menacing beacon of light hunting them—everything had changed. Even the air was different; it smelled musty, like an old quilt long forgotten at the bottom of a trunk .

She heard a slight movement nearby. "Nathan?"

"Yeah." His voice was a rough whisper. "Are you OK?"

"Pretty much." She pushed aside the hair hanging across her face; it was caked with webbing and grit like an old dust mop.

For several long seconds they both lay there speechless as the shock of the moment wore off and was replaced by the realization of what had happened.

"Saved by the door," Gina said at last, venting her nervous energy.

"A *secret* door," Nathan added

"What?"

Strength was slowly returning to his legs and he pushed himself up into a sitting position. "The chimera was the trigger for a secret door." He felt around in the dark for his backpack that slipped off his shoulder when he fell.

"The what?" she asked.

"You remember yesterday in the library? I was looking at some pictures when you came up behind me?" His hand brushed against the side of his pack and he leaned over and plucked it up off the floor. The effort sent a sliver of pain shooting through his forehead, but he worked through it—feeding off the excitement of their discovery.

"That was one of *those* things?" A twinge of apprehension stirred in the back of her mind.

"Yeah...we can talk about it later. But right now..." He unzipped the side compartment and pulled out an old metal tin. Inside were two tea candles and a small box of wooden matches.

"What are you doing?" Gina asked.

"You'll see." He fumbled with the match momentarily and a small yellow flame jumped to life. When he touched it to the wick, a slightly smaller but steady cone of white light appeared and he saw Gina sitting a few feet away. She was propped up, leaning on one arm like it was a crutch. Her hair was a tangled mess.

He moved the candle to his right and saw a giant slab of granite, draped with stringy cobwebs that sagged lifelessly towards the floor. It was the panel in the wall that had opened unexpectedly and sent them both tumbling onto the stone floor in rough fashion. The sight of the webs made him shudder, causing the candle flame to flicker.

"Where are we?" she asked, glancing around at the gloomy surroundings.

"In some kind of secret room."

She felt another flutter of nervousness as a startling thought surfaced in her mind. Just as quickly, and with equal resolve, she pushed it away—she wasn't willing to believe it yet. "A secret room for what?" Her heart began to beat faster, despite her attempts to remain calm.

Nathan didn't answer. He swung the candle slowly to his left and paused.

151

His jaw fell open.

It's not a room...

"You've got *what?*" the crane operator yelled to the foreman as they stood on the front steps of the courthouse. Behind them, a 300-ton crane idled noisily in the street, sending billows of pearl gray exhaust into the morning air.

The foreman hitched his thumb towards the front door. "Two kids...inside."

"What?" His eyes went wide. "What are two kids doing inside the building?"

"Beats me. They snuck in somehow."

The crane operator exhaled loudly. He motioned to his three-man crew, who were standing next to the crane, waiting to extend the outriggers.

"What are you doing?" the foreman demanded.

"Nothing," the crane operator shot back. "We don't move until you find those kids."

"NO," the foreman said, taking a step closer. "Get your crew moving...NOW...we're late enough as it is."

The crane operator stood his ground. "That's not my problem."

"Oh, there' s going to be a problem all right. Look, my men are searching for them right now," the foreman yelled. "They probably already found them."

"I don't see them...do you?"

The foreman looked away and spit.

"Let me know when you find them," the crane operator barked. He turned and marched down the steps, shaking his head in disbelief.

Nathan stared past the faint light of the candle at a long narrow void. It was obscured by layers of webbing that hung from the ceiling in thin sheets.

Oh great...spiders...

"What's that?" Gina asked.

"It's a passageway." He turned and handed her the candle. "Here...hold this."

"It's a *what?* Wait...what are you going to do?"

He scrambled to his feet and slipped on his backpack. "You mean what are WE going to do? His hands were trembling with excitement when he took the candle from her and turned towards the dense labyrinth of spider webs. "We're going to find out where this leads."

Even if we have to fight off a whole army of spiders.

"Hold on..." she started to say, "I think we should..."

But he wasn't listening. He took a deep breath and then stepped forward, pushing aside the webbing with a wide sweep of his arm.

"Nathan...WAIT!"

She hurried to her feet and closed in behind him, matching him step for step. They had only walked five feet when they were forced to stop and peel away gobs of webbing that clung to them head to foot. They continued on for several more feet, when Nathan stopped.

"Hey!" Gina blurted out as she collided with him. She quickly took a step back. "Sorry about that."

Nathan didn't respond. He didn't even turn around. He stood perfectly still, staring intently at the wall of stone that marked the end of the passageway. Something about it was different. He lifted the candle higher and stepped closer.

"What's wrong?" Gina asked, peeking over his shoulder. There was some sort of fuzzy object attached to the wall, but from where she was standing it was impossible to identify.

Nathan pulled away handfuls of webbing and the figure was slowly revealed: the piercing eyes, the gaping mouth with long curved fangs, a set of wings that loomed high over the shoulders, and the powerful arms, poised to strike with open, hooked claws. They were carved in pale gray stone with thin streaks of black that resembled swollen veins. Nathan gasped and his eyes went wide with dread. "What is it?" Gina whispered.

"Gargoyle," he replied in a dazed monotone.

Gina knew that voice. It was the same one he used in his father's office, when they were looking at the calendar.

"OK...come on," she said, tugging on his arm, "let's go back."

Nathan didn't budge. He stared at the gargoyle, ignoring her repeated attempts to pull him away. "No," he said in the same chilling voice, "this is it." He was mesmerized, because it all made sense now—the gargoyle that taunted him in his dreams, appearing repeatedly before his eyes—only to vanish into the mist. The dream was a clue, but he didn't realize its meaning until now.

Gina crossed her arms. Then she bit a knuckle on her fist. It was just like before, in his basement. Nothing she could say would break him out of his hypnotic trance. Something had control of him, and it wouldn't let go.

He reached out again and began peeling away more cobwebs. With each handful, more of the gargoyle's horrid features were exposed: the strands of torn flesh wedged between the teeth, carved in exacting detail, the curved hooks, like tiny barbs, protruding from each turn of the

154

wings; rows of serpentine scales running up and down its muscular legs that were bent at the knees.

"Uh...Nathan...we really should go back," Gina whimpered. He ignored her desperate plea and caressed the ghastly beast like a beloved house pet. "Wh-what are you doing?" she asked.

The candle flame flickered and jumped, making the gargoyle appear to move in response to his every touch.

"This is what he wanted us to find."

Gina couldn't stop her body from shaking. "Look Nathan, I'm serious...let's just get out of here...we can go up..."

"No," he said sharply, his mood growing more intense. "We're very close...I can feel it."

The cobwebs were completely gone now, but his hand continued to move gracefully over the gargoyle's face, searching every sharp jag and rounded edge. Dream images flashed in his mind like lightning strikes, and with each one the meaning became clearer. What he did next made Gina scream.

He reached into the gargoyle's mouth.

She lunged forward and grabbed his shoulders to pull him away just as the floor shifted beneath their feet. Through half-closed eyes she saw the darkness streak past in a jumbled blur of black, brown and gray, as they were thrown sideways with astonishing force.

Seconds later, a deathly silence filled the passageway. The silken webs that had ruffled briefly only seconds before, hung motionless once again. The tea candle lay spent on the cold stone floor.

Nathan and Gina were gone.

Chapter Eleven

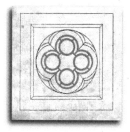

The Library

   Nathan lay on his back after being yanked backwards, as if caught in the grip of a giant hand and hurtled onto the cold stone floor with a jaw-rattling thud. His eyes blinked open and he stared into a wall of solid black.

Another secret space...

   The air was different here. It didn't smell as musty as the passageway, and it was slightly cooler. Ignoring the dull ache in his forehead, he sat up quickly and slipped the backpack off his shoulder. Seconds later a burst of light shattered the darkness as he lit his last tea candle and lifted it up in the air with unsteady hands—its pearl white glow falling across the stone gargoyle on the near wall. In the broken light it loomed over him like a silent guardian.

   Gina was lying on her side a few feet away, rubbing the small lump on the back of her head. When she heard the match ignite, she rolled over on her back and lifted a hand to shield her eyes from the jarring light. "What *is* that?" Her voice was fuzzy, like she'd been shaken out of a deep sleep.

"A second door," Nathan answered, awestruck, as he quickly stood up and moved closer to examine it. A pencil-thin seam in the wall formed a wide, rectangular outline around the gargoyle. It was choked with broken cobwebs that were pulled into the gap when the wall opened and then closed.

"Another secret door," she whispered. The doubts she'd clung to throughout the week, about Nathan's mysterious quest and his fascination with Alastair Raven, were melting away. Not one hidden door, but two? A secret passageway? None of it was normal. People didn't construct such things unless they were hiding something.

"This door was different." He looked down at the floor below the gargoyle's feet and saw the semicircular stone pedestal where he and Gina had stood just moments earlier.

"What do you mean?" She eased herself upright with both hands.

"The first door swung open," he said. "This one spun around when my hand hit the lever."

"What lever?"

"The one in the gargoyle's mouth."

"Oh…*that's* what you were doing."

"It's a long story," he mumbled, remembering the horrifying image from his dream where the gargoyle snaps his arm off. It was a portion of his nightmare that required no further interpretation.

Gina started to get up off the floor and then paused. "That's different." She was running her hands back and forth over the floor.

"What did you say?"

"The floor…it feels different…"

Nathan hobbled over to where she was sitting and held the candle low to the floor. Unlike the rough stone floor of the passageway, this was a repeating pattern of polished tiles. In the dim light they were mottled shades of gray and white and resembled gathering storm clouds. "They look like marble," he said, moving the candle over them. He was tracing the pattern across the floor towards the wall when he stopped abruptly and lifted the candle into the air. "Whoa...look at this."

Gina scrambled to her feet and hurried over to join him. The wall was covered with miniature tiles in various colors, each no bigger than a postage stamp. They formed a grand circular mosaic that was at least eight feet wide. Nathan recognized it immediately from his reading.

"A Rose window," he whispered as he passed the candle back and forth slowly in front of it, closely inspecting the intricate details.

Gina wasn't sure she heard him correctly.

"That's a *window*?"

"No," he said, running his fingertips slowly over the uneven surface, "this is either a design for one or the copy of a real one somewhere."

He explained how the window design got its name, pointing out the mullions that radiated outward from the center roundel and formed the image of a flower, and the quatrefoils and trefoils that ringed the outer edge.

When he was done, she let out a heavy breath and surveyed the darkness around them.

"What is this place?" Her voice an equal mix of fear and astonishment.

"Let's find out. He stepped around her and extended the candle further down the wall.

"What is that?" she asked, looking past him into the void.

"It looks like a hallway."

They crept towards the opening that was at least ten feet wide. It was framed on both sides with elaborate wrought iron brackets that extended out from the wall. They were identical in shape, dipping down slightly and then turning upward with a series of ornate motifs fashioned along the top and bottom. On the end of each bracket was a shallow cup-like candleholder. The candles, or what was left of them, were just mountainous globs of wax.

"Ewww," Gina said.

"They're just candles," Nathan replied very matter-of-factly.

"Yeah, but what happened to them?"

He leaned closer and inspected the perimeter, where once hot wax had broken through the folds and dripped down onto the floor. "Looks like it burned out." He lowered the candle and saw slender pinnacles of wax rising up in the darkness like a skeleton's long boney fingers.

Further down the wall they found an identical set, one on each side of the hallway. "That's odd," he said, examining what was left of the wax.

"What?"

"Uh…nothing," he replied, moving along quickly until he came to a junction where the corridor made a slight turn to the right. He took two steps and stopped short.

"What is it?" Gina asked.

He stood speechless, mesmerized by the large recessed sections in the wall on both sides of the corridor. Each was set between two spectacular columns, carved from speckled granite, with a ceiling formed from arched diagonal ribbing. "Ribbed vaults," he whispered.

He'd seen several versions in Compton's Journal, but none as elaborate as these. They walked past them slowly, in awed silence, looking from side to side. Each vault was more stunning than the one before, and affixed to the wall between them was another wrought iron bracket, encased in melted wax.

Gina stopped in front of one pillar and looked up at the top. It was carved with an ornate floral design that resembled a thicket of leafy vines.

"Those are called capitals," Nathan said.

"They're beautiful," she said, staring at the intricate carving. For the first time since Nathan showed her the book from the attic, she was glad that he'd taken the time to read it. But she wasn't ready to share that with him. Maybe when they got safely out of the building.

Beyond the majestic ribbed vaults was another junction where the corridor made another turn to the right.

Gina gasped and then covered her mouth.

Running down both sides of the corridor were massive arched openings, set back from the walkway by three heavy stone steps. A thick rounded pillar separated each one, which was then divided into two identical smaller arches by a slightly smaller matching pillar.

"Balustrades," Nathan said, holding the candle high up in the air. They stood over ten feet tall, and he had to crane his neck to see the fine detail of the trefoil arch atop each one.

"Look at *those* capitals," Gina said, pointing at one set of pillars. They were slightly tapered and finely carved with broad leaves that curled outwards.

Halfway down the corridor, Nathan stopped. One of the balustrades on the outer wall was different than the others.

"Look at this," he nearly shouted.

161

The partition in the back was missing. He stepped forward with the candle and saw a steep, narrow stairway.

"What did you find?"

"It looks like a way out."

The foreman trudged up the stairs to the lobby, cursing aloud with every step. He'd been up and down the hallway for the past twenty minutes, searching every square inch of the walls and floor for any kind of hidden door or crawlspace. All he found was solid stone and airtight seams.

When he reached the top of the stairs, he saw one of his workmen coming down the adjacent stairway from the second floor. "What'd you find?" he asked in a rough tone.

"Nothing," the worker replied. "We checked this floor *and* upstairs...those kids are gone."

The foreman gritted his teeth and growled. "We should be so lucky." He glanced down the stairs at the lower level momentarily, then turned and looked over at the front door. "Did anyone check outside?"

"I don't think so

"Do it now," the foreman said. "Check the perimeter of the building. See if you can find any place where they might've snuck out."

"OK." The worker turned and walked briskly across the lobby to the front door, happy to exit the gloom and emerge into the sunshine. With any luck he could bum a cigarette from one of his buddies.

Nathan and Gina carefully stepped through the opening of the balustrade and followed the narrow stairway up to a small landing. From there the stairway turned and continued up a second flight of stairs where it stopped at another landing.

162

Light was streaming in from the outside, through a series of small repeating diamond shapes in the wall. The shadow they cast on the floor below looked like a giant honeycomb.

"What is this?" Gina asked.

"It's a type of grille work," Nathan replied, extinguishing the candle. "It's called diaper pattern." He held his hand up to one of the openings and felt a steady stream of warm air caress his fingers. The rumble of an idling engine lingered in the distance.

"That's a funny name."

He didn't reply as he bent down to look through one of the openings. This was a vent—not a door—and as he breathed in the fresh morning air, he knew they'd have to find another way to sneak out of the building.

"What are you looking at?" Gina asked.

"See for yourself."

She ducked down and looked through one of the diagonal openings. Across the alley that separated the two buildings, she saw a cinder block wall bathed in sunlight—the side of Owens Hardware. The sunlight vanished when a man's face appeared on the other side of the grille work, just inches away from hers.

"HEY," he shouted.

They both stumbled backwards and fell onto the floor. As they lay in the shadows with their hearts pounding, Nathan put his finger to his lips and signaled...*QUIET!*

The man moved to another section and yelled again. "HEY."

Then came the sound of a second voice. "Ronnie!"

The first man turned away from the grille. "Hey Jimmy, you got a smoke?"

Gina started to move towards the steps, but Nathan grabbed her arm and motioned with his other hand...*DON'T MOVE!*

Jimmy came into view and offered Ronny a cigarette. "What are you doin' over here?"

"Not much," Ronny scoffed, "Foster has me out here looking for those two brats we cornered in the basement."

Nathan heard the metallic clink of a lighter, and seconds later the rancid smell of cigarette smoke wafted in through the grille. He and Gina covered their mouths with their shirtsleeves.

"You *still* haven't found them?"

"Nope." Ronny took a drag off his cigarette and exhaled. "Foster's about to lose it," he chuckled. "I don't think he's gonna wait much longer."

"You think he'd...?"

"As mad as he is? I wouldn't put it past him."

"What a moron," Jimmy said. "Hey, I better get back out front. I'll talk to you later."

"Yeah, see ya later."

Ronny snuffed out his cigarette against the side of the building and flicked it through the grille work. Nathan's eyes followed it as it flew just inches from his head and landed softly behind him in the shadows.

When they were sure he was gone, they eased back down the stairs to the first landing.

"That was close," Gina said with a sigh of relief.

"Yeah, tell me about it," Nathan replied, taking the box of matches out of his backpack.

"The way he yelled, I thought he saw us."

"Nah...I think he was just listening to the echo."

He lit the candle and the landing was instantly bathed in a soft light that threw their shadows high on the near wall.

"What did he mean by...?" Gina began.

"I'm not sure," Nathan said, cutting her off. He started down the steps. "Come on, we need to keep moving."

They set off back down to the corridor and continued past the last balustrade. There, the corridor took another slight turn and they both stopped walking. For several seconds they stood without speaking, staring into the murky shadows.

"Anything?" Foster asked, when Ronny strolled into the front lobby.

"Not a thing."

"And you checked the whole perimeter?"

"Everywhere."

Foster's face twisted in anger. "That does it," he said, through clenched teeth as he pushed past Ronny. He stormed towards the front door and yelled, "Clear the building."

Nathan and Gina stood in the corridor, staring into a large room that was at least twelve feet deep and twenty four feet across.

"What is it?" Gina asked.

"I'm not sure," Nathan replied as he stepped into the room and raised the candle up in the air, "but it looks like a library." The outer walls were lined with chest-high bookcases filled with hardcover volumes, antiquated hand tools, and curious pieces of carved stone. Sitting in the middle of the room was a long wooden table, covered with a thick layer of dust. Something about it drew Nathan's immediate attention. "It's strange," he said.

"What's strange?"

"There aren't any chairs."

"Look," Gina said, pointing at two heavy brass candleholders that sat several inches apart on the table. Each one held a long slender candlestick, and unlike the candles they'd seen earlier, these were intact. Nathan hurried over at once and lit them.

"What are those?" Gina asked. She was pointing at a small pile of granite blocks mounded into a neat pile between the candleholders. Each was no larger than a hockey puck.

"No idea," Nathan said, handing Gina one of the brass candleholders.

She took it and turned to the bookcases along the outer wall. "These books are ancient."

"They should be," Nathan replied, moving slowly along the row of bookcases towards the far corner of the room, "think of how long they've..."

He stopped.

The light from his candle fell across something on the end wall—an enormous wooden container, centered between two of the bookcases. It was hard to miss, at four feet high and over five feet wide. It extended out from the wall nearly four feet, atop a thick wooden base. At first glance it looked like a bureau, but there were no drawers; just two square split panel doors, held shut by a thick brass hasp.

Sitting on the top were two small candleholders made from hammered copper. Their short candles leaked hardened wax down the sides and into the shallow saucer-like bases.

"What's wrong?" Gina asked, from the opposite side of the room.

"Check this out."

166

"What is it?" She glanced over and saw the massive wooden case illuminated in the broad pocket of light from his candle.

"Not sure, but I'm about to find out."

"Wait," she blurted out. She hurried over and stood next to him as he flipped the hasp and slowly opened both doors. It took him a moment to realize what he was seeing.

"Whoa..."

The case was filled with small cubbies, roughly four inches square. A thick roll of paper was visible in each one, with the exception of a few empty cubbies along the bottom. Before Gina could ask what they were, he gingerly slid one of the rolls out and took it over to the center table.

It was almost four feet long and several sheets thick. Using great care he slowly unrolled it, the brittle paper creaking softly with every turn, until his arms were stretched out wide in each direction, struggling to keep it flat.

"Wait a second," Gina said. She hurried over to the middle of the table and grabbed four pieces of granite from the stack. "Use these."

Nathan stared at the pile of granite for a moment, then looked over at the open case.

Of course...

They put one block of stone on each corner of the sheet and then moved their candles closer.

"Is that what I think it is?" Gina asked.

"These are blueprints," Nathan replied, scanning the faded writing and the depiction of a large stone building. He turned back the first page and saw more detailed drawings. "Unbelievable."

"Do you recognize that building?" Gina asked.

"It looks like the library."

"I think you're right."

Nathan pointed to the bottom right hand corner of the paper. "And look who the builder was."

Gina looked down and saw the same two initials they'd seen on the front of the building earlier in the week.

AV

"It's him," she said, awestruck.

"That's right...but we know who he *really* is."

His heart was pounding when he looked over at her, his eyes wide with realization and excitement. "This is it," he exclaimed, "this is what he wanted us to find."

Gina stared back with equal astonishment, nodding her head slowly.

He's right...

The stunning realization left her speechless.

He was right all along.

The thought that a book had brought them this far was beyond her realm of comprehension. Even more astounding was the fact that Nathan Cole had read it. That alone qualified as a miracle, and she eyed him with a newfound appreciation.

They looked through more cubbies and found other buildings and monuments they recognized. With each passing minute, the impact of their discovery became bigger and bigger, and before long the table was covered with blueprints. It was more than either of them could have imagined.

"Look at all of these," Nathan said, pointing to the rows of cubbies in the case. "He didn't vanish...he kept working."

"This is incredible" Gina replied. "We need to tell someone about it." There was a tone of urgency in her voice.

Nathan turned away from the case. "You said you saw a crane outside?"

"Yeah, it was coming up the street when I snuck in the front door."

"I didn't see the crane," he said, "but I *did* see dump trucks and a bunch of men waiting around. I thought they were getting ready to pave the road."

Gina rolled her eyes. "They don't set up roadblocks when they pave."

"I never thought of that," Nathan said, shaking his head as he spoke. "I was in a hurry to get here...too busy thinking about how I was going to get inside..."

"So what are we going to do?"

"Whatever they're planning to do, we need to stop them," he said, thinking about the historical importance of what they'd found.

"But how?"

Nathan shut the doors of the case. "We have to get outside...and fast...we need to tell them what we found."

"Too bad we can't use that stairway." Gina said, referring to the balustrade.

"Yeah, I know," he sighed, tapping his fingers anxiously on the top of the case. He bit the edge of his lip, trying to think of what to do. Finally, he let out a heavy breath. "We'll just have to go out the way we came in."

"Wait...what?"

He grabbed the two short candleholders from the top of the case. "You take this," he said. "I'll save this one as a backup...just in case."

He lit Gina's candle and they hurried out of the library. The revolving stone door with the gargoyle was less than twenty feet away. As they walked towards it they passed a section of wall that was covered by a heavy velvet curtain.

"What's this?" Gina asked as she walked past it. Before Nathan could respond, she grabbed the curtain and pulled it aside.

The scream that followed echoed through the entire corridor. Nathan snatched the candle from her hand as she teetered momentarily and then collapsed on the floor.

"GINA!"

Foster was standing at the front door as the last of his men exited the building.

"Everyone out?" he asked.

"All clear," the worker replied. He walked down the front steps and joined the other men on the sidewalk.

The crane operator was halfway up the front steps when he yelled, "What are you doing?"

"My job," Foster yelled back.

"No you're not," the crane operator said, shaking his head. He charged up the steps to the doorway and stopped just inches from Foster's face. "Where are those kids?"

"Gone," Foster barked.

"How do you know?"

"I don't answer to you," Foster bellowed. The two men were chest to chest, neither one willing to back down. Just then, one of the workers raced up the steps.

"Hey boss," he yelled to Foster.

Foster continued to stare at the crane operator for several more seconds, his face flush with anger, then he turned to the worker. "What is it?"

"There's something you gotta see."

Gina was propped up on the floor, shaking uncontrollably, when Nathan knelt down to check on her. "No...no..." she kept repeating. Her eyes, wide open in shock, turned away from the curtain, refusing to look at it.

"What is it?" he asked, nodding towards the curtain. "Is something in *there*?"

She put up her hand, trying to push it all away—far away.

Nathan stood up and walked over to the curtain. When he pulled it back, he opened it so only he could see beyond it.

The room was very small. Just inside, pushed up against the wall, was a massive roll-top desk. Sitting at the swivel chair, slumped forward onto the desktop was a human skeleton.

An icy jolt gripped his entire body. The skull was resting on the left arm of the skeleton's body, while the right arm dangled down over the side of the chair in defeat. A ragged outfit hung loosely from its bones, dotted with large moth-eaten holes that exposed the dull white bones beneath the cloth.

The sight of the body, and the foul stench emanating from the room, made Nathan let go of the curtain and turn away. He clenched his teeth and covered his mouth, fighting the impulse to throw up.

Gina grabbed his leg. "Help me up." He reached down and pulled her up with one hand, and they stumbled over to the revolving door. When they were directly in front of the gargoyle, Nathan stepped onto the pedestal.

"OK...here's what we have to do," he said, still shaken from the hideous sight they had just witnessed. "You stand behind me and hold on... *tight*."

"Yeah, yeah...that part I know," she said.

"I'll extinguish the candle and then pull the lever. When we get to the other side, I'll relight it. OK?"

Gina took a deep breath. "OK."

She stepped forward and put both arms around his waist. Seconds later she closed her eyes and everything went sideways. When she opened her eyes again, she and Nathan were still standing on the pedestal, but the air felt stagnant and moldy; she knew they were back in the passageway.

"You OK?" he asked, letting go of the gargoyle.

"Yeah...it wasn't so bad the second time."

Working quickly in the dark, he dug out the matches and lit the candle. "All right." He took a deep breath and then let it out. "Let's go."

The light from the candle filled the narrow passageway as he stepped forward and pushed through the stringy webs. *We're almost out,* he kept telling himself.

One last obstacle remained.

"One of the guys just found their bikes," the workman said as he and Foster walked down the steps. The crane operator followed close behind them, step for step. When they reached the sidewalk, the workman led Foster over to the small patch of dead grass next to the steps. A pair of kids' bikes were lying awkwardly on the ground, thrown there without regard. Foster took one look at them and swore.

"Where did you find them?"

"Over there," the crew member replied, nodding down the street, "in the alley."

Foster turned and looked. "Wait, you found them over *there*?" He was pointing down the street.

"Some of the guys did, yeah."

"They could belong to *anyone*."

The crane operator shook his head. "No," he said, staring at Foster, who obviously didn't know the first thing about kids. "No kid would leave his bike behind." He pointed up at the courthouse. "They're still in there somewhere."

When Nathan and Gina reached the end of the passageway, they saw a faint impression on the wall, where the spider webs had been disturbed when the stone partition opened.

"So how do we get it to open?" Gina asked.

Nathan shrugged. "I have no idea. It was sheer luck that it opened from the other side, but there *has* to be some way to open it from this side." He took the second candleholder out of his backpack and lit it for Gina. "I'll check this side," he said, motioning to the right side of the door, "you check that side."

Gina turned and quickly began searching the wall.

This is better than a word puzzle.

She raised the candle up near the ceiling and slowly worked her way down, trying to envision what she might find.

A lever?

The stone was partially obscured by webs.

A button?

She pulled them aside, studying every break in the stone.

A switch?

It could be anything.

Meanwhile, Nathan was busy moving the candle up and down the wall by the seam of the door, carefully inspecting every square inch. If there was an opening mechanism, it had to be close by. There was no way Raven would have left out

173

that detail, unless he had constructed another hidden door that they'd missed. He searched faster, hoping he was wrong.

Gina exhaled loudly. She was halfway down the wall and hadn't found anything. Perhaps her detective skills didn't work so well in dusty, dark, secret rooms. She passed the candle back and forth in desperation, her eyes darting back and forth with every pass, but she saw only lifeless stone and matted strands of age-old spider webs. When she reached the floor, something caught her eye. She reached out to touch it.

A few feet away, Nathan was running his hands over the rough stone when he felt something give. It was a small section of wall, no bigger than the end of a brick, buried beneath the webs. He touched it again and the massive door swung open with a dull scraping sound. Gina was kneeling on the floor and jumped out of the way the second she saw it start to move. Moments later they were in the dark basement hallway, running for the stairs that led to the first floor lobby.

Foster was walking back up the steps when Nathan and Gina came charging out the front door. When he looked up and saw them racing towards him, covered in spider webs and filth, he missed the step and fell forward onto the stairs, grinding his elbow into the hard stone. Nathan and Gina saw the crane positioned in front of the building and ran right past him, straight towards the crane operator.

"YOU HAVE TO STOP!" Nathan yelled, over the growl of the idling engine.

Foster climbed to his feet and came storming back down the steps.

"GRAB THOSE KIDS," he shouted to the crane operator, "HOLD 'EM RIGHT THERE!"

174

The crane operator ignored him and tried to hear what Nathan was saying.

"TAKE IT EASY KID," he said. "WHAT'S WRONG?"

Just then Foster charged at them and tried to grab Nathan by the back of the shirt.

"HEY," the crane operator yelled, stepping in front of Nathan at the last second to keep Foster from getting to him. "LEAVE 'EM ALONE."

Foster stopped in his tracks, and for several seconds neither man moved. Behind them, the mechanical growl of the crane's engine thundered up and down the street.

"YOU HAVE TO STOP," Nathan shouted, tugging on the back of the crane operator's shirt.

"WHY?" he asked, turning slightly without giving Foster room to get by. He could see the look of desperation on Nathan's face. Something was really bothering the kid.

"Oh for crying out loud," Foster yelled. "I'M CALLING THE COPS."

He stormed over to his truck as Nathan pleaded with the crane operator.

"THERE'S A BODY INSIDE."

"IN THE BASEMENT," Gina added.

"A BODY?" the crane operator asked, "WHAT KIND OF BODY?"

"A HUMAN BODY," Nathan and Gina shouted at the same time.

"ARE YOU SURE?"

Nathan and Gina nodded their heads frantically.

"SHOW ME," the crane operator said.

Further down the street, Foster was standing next to his truck talking on his two-way radio. He did a double take when he looked over and saw the crane operator walking up the steps with the two kids. When the three of them disappeared into the building, he threw the handset down on the seat and raced up the stairs after them.

Chapter Twelve

The Vearn Trust

Chuck Gerard walked into his editor's office at the *Metro West Times*, eyes glued to a magazine folded open in his hands. "Hey Frank, did you see the..."

Frank's hand shot up in the air, signaling Chuck to stop. He was perched over his desk, listening to the garbled voice coming from a small police scanner.

"Copy 809...confirm 10-54 at that address."

The radio went silent and Frank pulled open the top drawer of his desk, rifling through the mess until he found a well-worn list of police radio codes. He ran his finger down the column of numbers until he came to 10-54. "Possible dead body."

"Where?" Gerard asked.

Frank turned down the volume on the scanner. "The old courthouse."

"The old courthouse?" Chuck asked with a look of disbelief. "But that place has been locked up tight for..."

"Yeah, yeah, I know," Frank said, "and it was scheduled to be demolished today."

"I smell a front page story."

"Me too. Can you go down there and check it out?"

"Sure."

"You better hurry. I'm guessing it's going to be a three-ring circus."

Chuck spun around and hurried towards the door.

"AND DON'T FORGET YOUR CAMERA," Frank yelled as Gerard ducked out into the hallway.

Nathan and Gina were sitting on the sidewalk between the Courthouse and Owens Hardware. The crane operator sat between them. The roar of the crane's engine had long since stopped and his crew stood nearby, smoking cigarettes and watching the whole situation unfold.

"So...are you guys OK?" he asked. Despite what they had told him earlier, they looked pretty rough around the edges.

"Yeah, just a little sore," Gina said with a grimace, twisting her body slightly.

"I think my headache is finally gone," Nathan added. He touched the side of his head and then inspected his fingertips for blood—he saw nothing but spider webs.

Several feet away, the first policeman on the scene, Officer Briggs, was sitting in his cruiser. He had been on his radio ever since they came out of the courthouse ten minutes earlier. When he saw an ambulance turn the corner at the far end of the street, with its light bar flashing, he quickly climbed out of the cruiser.

"Here we go," the crane operator said, standing up. He signaled to the ambulance and then turned back to Nathan and Gina. "The EMTs are going to look you over and make sure you're OK, so I'll say goodbye and see about getting that crane out of here."

"Thank you for helping us," Gina said.

"Don't mention it. Just think what we would have destroyed," he said with a smile. He motioned to Briggs that he was leaving and then walked back up the street.

The ambulance stopped in front of Nathan and Gina and two EMTs climbed out of the cab. They spoke with Officer Briggs for almost a minute, with one of them jotting down notes on a small pad of paper. When they were finished, the EMT with the notepad came over to the curb. "I hear you two have had quite a morning," he said. He knelt down in front of them, taking inventory of the small cuts and scratches on their faces.

"Yeah," Nathan exclaimed. He looked over at the crane and felt a wave of relief, thinking about Raven's secret rooms and how close they came to being destroyed forever.

"My name is Carter," the EMT said, "what's your name?"

"Nathan Cole."

"Hello, Nathan. And your name?" Carter asked, looking at Gina.

"Gina McDermott."

Carter checked his notes briefly and nodded, "Hello, Gina." Then he looked at each of them alternately. "Do you know where you are?"

"Yes," Gina said, trying very hard not to giggle. "We're downtown." She shot Nathan a quick smirk. *Duh.*

"How about you, Nathan?"

"Sure," he said, wondering if it was a trick question. "We're sitting on the curb next to the courthouse."

If only the tests at school were this easy.

"Very good," Carter said with an approving nod. "Do you know what day it is?"

"Saturday," They both replied at the same time.

"That's right." Then he looked at Gina and asked, "What happened here?"

"You mean in there?" She answered, nodding towards the courthouse.

"Uh-huh," Carter said, watching her eyes as she spoke. She looked alert but he had to be sure.

"Well," Gina began, "we were downstairs in the basement..."

"And it was pitch black..." Nathan blurted out.

Gina shot him an angry look. *Let me finish.* "We were trying to find a way to get outside..."

"And we found a secret passageway..." Gina elbowed him in the side. "And some hidden rooms." Before Nathan could interrupt again, she quickly added, "and a *skeleton*." She looked over at Nathan and beamed. *Ha ha.*

"OK, OK," Carter said, convinced that they were both more than alert and oriented. He opened his medical bag and took out a stethoscope, along with another contraption that neither of them recognized.

"A secret passageway...hidden rooms...that sounds pretty scary," Carter mused as he slipped on the stethoscope and then wrapped an inflation cuff around Nathan's upper arm.

"Too many spiders," Nathan said.

"I'll bet," Carter replied, his eyes glued to his watch as he took Nathan's blood pressure. When he was done, he removed the cuff from Nathan's arm and repeated the process with Gina.

Chuck Gerard got within two blocks of the courthouse when he saw an army of policemen and police cars clogging the street up ahead—they had the road blocked off and weren't letting anyone through. Thinking quickly, he swerved into the parking lot of the dry cleaner, grabbed his notepad and jumped out of the car.

One block up was Franklin Street, a street he knew all too well.. Years ago he'd written a feature story on the original buildings that used to line the street, many built before the turn of the century. Their architectural beauty had been destroyed, only to be replaced by walls of dull brick and cold storefront windows. One thing remained from the original layout of the street—an old alley that connected Franklin Street to Court Street.

He raced to the corner of Franklin and paused long enough to look down the street, at the opening of the alley.

All clear.

The street in front of the courthouse was a whirlwind of activity and the squawk of police radios filled the air. The ambulance was moved to make room for the crane, which roared to life again and inched its way down the street. Foster and his crew gathered their gear, piled into their trucks and drove off.

Police barricades were quickly set up at both ends of the street, to control the growing mob of curious onlookers. All non-essential traffic was diverted away from the scene. Another barricade was set up in front of the courthouse steps and only approved personnel were allowed inside the building.

Nathan and Gina were taking it all in when they looked over and saw Officer Briggs walking towards them. He wasn't alone.

"NATHAN?"

"GINA?"

"Uh-oh," Gina said, "we've had it now."

Nathan let out a heavy sigh, shaking his head back and forth. "You can say that again."

"Those must be your parents," Carter said, as he packed up his medical equipment.

Nathan and Gina both nodded gravely.

"Let me handle this," he said with a wink.

Gerard ducked into the alley completely unnoticed. Minutes later he reached the other end, where he paused momentarily to peek around the corner. To his left, a short distance away, an ambulance sat parked near the curb. Across from it, on the opposite side of the street, an EMT was examining two kids who looked like they'd crawled through a mile-long trash heap.

The seasoned reporter slipped out of the alley and walked quickly up the sidewalk to the ambulance. He heard the commotion before he even got there.

Carter stood up and intercepted the parents.

"Your kids are fine," he assured them, holding up both palms in a calming gesture. "And I'm sure you have questions..."

"You bet we do," Gina's father bellowed, stepping around Carter. He stormed over to Gina, his face burning with anger. "What were you thinking...coming down here?"

Before she could answer, Gina's mother intervened. "And why would the two of you even *think* of going into such a dreadful building?"

"It's not dreadful," Gina said, "it's amazing."

"I wouldn't call a dead body 'amazing,'" her father replied in a sharp tone.

"Before you get into that," Carter said, trying to ease the situation, "I need to explain something to you." He reached into his medical bag and took out a clipboard. "Ordinarily, we would take Nathan and Gina to the hospital for further tests, but I don't think that's necessary. Other than a few scrapes, like I said before, I think they're fine. But I do need you to sign this." He extended the clipboard to Gina's father, who took it and scanned it hastily from top to bottom.

"What is this?" he asked, impatiently.

"It's a release form."

"Release?"

Carter took the next few minutes to explain the reason for the form, citing standard procedures for the medical response team. While he was doing that, Nathan's mother looked down at him and mouthed...*Are you OK?*

Nathan smiled and shrugged his shoulders.

Of course.

The EMT had the group completely distracted.

"Perfect," Gerard whispered.

He eased around the end of the ambulance and casually strolled across the street in their direction, taking his time and trying not to draw attention to himself.

By the time Carter had the signatures he needed, Gina's parents had cooled down considerably.

183

"Now," Nathan's father asked, "will someone *please* tell me what this is all about?"

"Thank you," Gina's father added. "The police said something about hidden rooms? A dead body? It sounds like a zombie movie for crying out loud."

"Actually," Nathan said, looking over his shoulder at the courthouse, "this is going to be huge."

His mother eyed him suspiciously. "What do you mean, Nathan?"

"I've been studying the man who built this building," he said, with a quick glance at Gina. "We both have."

"So that would explain *this*?" his father quipped, pulling Nathan's note from his back pocket and waving it in the air. He pursed his lips and tilted his head to one side, waiting for the fantastic excuse Nathan would try to put past them.

"Well...um...that was..." Nathan stammered. His parents looked at each other and smirked. *Same old Nathan.*

"His name was Alastair Raven," Gina blurted out, trying to change the subject as quickly as possible. "He was from New York City."

"And he was famous," Nathan added.

A small crowd began to gather around them as he explained Raven's education, his apprenticeship and the numerous buildings he'd designed in New York City, many of which were celebrated landmarks. He explained how the Gothic Revival led to the Classical Revival, which ushered in the twentieth century, and how Raven had become one of the most celebrated builders of his day.

All four parents were speechless.

Then he explained how Raven had suddenly vanished. As he told it, quoting the book (anonymously), "it remained one of the greatest architectural mysteries of all time."

184

After that, Gina told them about the information they learned from the town clerk, and how she used her word game to uncover the alias that Raven used while he worked right here in their town.

By this time all four parents were stunned, and they looked over at the courthouse, a look of astonishment on each of their faces.

"So this building has important historical value," said a deep, unknown voice. Everyone turned and looked at the older man who had wedged himself into the group, holding a small spiral notepad in one hand and a pen in the other. He had been frantically scribbling everything Nathan and Gina said, trying to keep up. Half the pages of his notepad were now jam-packed with notes.

"And you are?" Nathan's mother asked, eyeing his brown tweed sport coat and closely-cropped salt and pepper beard. He looked like one of her old college professors.

"Chuck Gerard," he replied with a nod. "*Metro West Times.*"

Nathan and Gina shared a look of utter surprise.

The newspaper?

Would they have their pictures taken? Would they be on the front page of the paper? What would their friends at school say?

Gerard stepped closer and asked, "You were saying...about the building?"

Nathan shook off his daydream. "It has *tons* of historical value. You should see the stuff inside, it's like a museum."

Another voice cut in from behind. "Which is why I'm revoking the demolition order effective immediately."

The booming voice came from a stocky man in a dark blue pinstripe suit as he pushed his way to the front of the group.

185

"As mayor, I can do that, you see," he said, stepping closer to shake Nathan's hand, then Gina's. "I'd say this city owes you both a huge debt of gratitude."

"The architectural community will have something to say about it as well," Gerard chimed in.

The mayor, who had dealt with Gerard on numerous occasions, nodded his enthusiastic agreement and then looked over at the courthouse. "To think, we were ready to knock it down…"

"That would have been a big mistake," Nathan said.

"Indeed," the mayor replied.

Just then, two other men stepped forward. The first one looked like Coach Gilbert from school, tall and muscular, and was dressed in a plain brown suit and patterned tie. The bright morning sun reflected off the gold police badge that was clipped to his top pocket. The second man looked more like Mr. Ellsworth, the wiry history teacher with gray hair and thin wire-rim glasses.

"Nathan? I'm Detective Ferguson," he said, "and this is Dr. Curtis. He's the County Medical Examiner. Do you mind if we talk to you for a few minutes?"

"No problem," Nathan said, standing up. That was four newcomers in as many minutes.

"Actually we'd like to speak with *both* of you," he said, looking directly at Gina.

Gina stood up next to Nathan as Ferguson took out a small notepad and pen. Dr. Curtis stood next to him without speaking—he was holding a thin black portfolio by his side.

"You've been very busy today," Ferguson said with a smile.

"Yeah," Nathan and Gina said at nearly the same time.

"I think you two might be able to help us piece this thing together. Think you can do that?"

"Sure," Gina said.

"What do you want to know?" Nathan asked.

Ferguson opened his notepad and read silently for a moment, reviewing the information he had collected from Officer Briggs and others at the scene. Then he looked at Nathan and asked, "How exactly did you find the body?"

"It was kind of an accident," Nathan explained, "once we discovered the secret chamber."

"How do you mean?" Ferguson asked.

"Actually, I discovered it when I opened the curtain," Gina said. "It looked funny just hanging on the wall, and I had no idea it was covering the entrance to a room. When I pulled it back I saw it sitting there...the skeleton I mean."

Gerard was so busy scribbling in his notepad that he didn't have time to look up. *Secret chamber?* This was too good.

"We were trying to find our way out of the building at the time," Nathan added.

"Did either of you go into the room?" Dr. Curtis asked, speaking up for the first time, "the room where the skeleton was?"

"No way," Gina replied with a shudder.

"We got out of there as fast as we could," Nathan said.

"So let me see if I have this right. You saw the curtain closed...you opened it...you saw the skeleton...and then you left?" Dr. Curtis asked.

"Uh-huh," Gina said.

"Was there anyone else with you?" Ferguson asked.

"Nope," Nathan replied.

"In the room with the skeleton?"

"No, it was just us," Gina said.

187

The next question came from Nathan. It was haunting him ever since they left the basement. Now, the one person who could answer it was standing right in front of him.

"The body…or actually the *skeleton*…" he asked, "is it…you know…?"

"The missing architect?" Ferguson asked, checking his notes, "Uh…Raven?"

Nathan nodded his head.

"Based on the initial evidence we found in the room," Dr. Curtis said, "and from what you just told us…yes, we have reason to believe that it's him. Of course, I'll be doing a full analysis of the remains, which will take several days."

Nathan felt his entire body tremble as he sat back down on the curb. Gina sat down next to him and patted his shoulder. "It's ok," she whispered.

Nathan sat there dazed, his face frozen in a blank stare, as the entire ordeal flashed through his mind. It started with a box of old dishes and ended with the skeleton of Alastair Raven collapsed on the desk. "It was him," he whispered, barely able to speak, "we found him."

Gina looked up at Dr. Curtis and asked, "How did he die?"

"Hard to say, really. A forensic team will do a full examination of the room, but we may never know for sure. Given the timeframe, my guess would be tuberculosis, or pneumonia." Then he stepped forward and handed something to Nathan."We found this on the desk."

"What is it?" Nathan asked.

"The letter he was writing when he died."

Nathan took the paper, handling it as if it might crumble into dust at any moment. It had yellowed with age and the corners were curled, but the handwriting was still legible.

He pushed the hair out of his face and began to read.

Reader,

I have been unwell all the day
and I fear my final hour is at hand.
Whatever circumstance gave you opportunity
to acquire this letter has consequently
revealed my hidden chambers,
for which I maintain a preference.

Nathan stopped reading and looked over at Gina. The color had drained from his face and his eyes were wide with shock.

"What does it say?" she asked.

"Take a look." She moved closer so they could read it while their parents and the others looked on.

All around them, the mayhem on the street continued. Law enforcement personnel came and went, reporters with camera crews roamed the street, interviewing anyone with information, or a comment, and still, the throng of onlookers continued to grow.

Nathan and Gina paid no attention to any of it. All they could hear was the voice of Alastair Raven.

In this sanctuary, after a life spent in labor,

189

I have found divergence from those who disgrace
the profession of architecture. I have hitherto had
to endure their greed and deception and
   bear witness to the defeat of
      many kindred spirits.

Gina stopped reading and whispered to Nathan.
"Is that why he vanished?"
"I think so," Nathan whispered as he kept reading, "look at this."

Under false appearance of another
who lived by habit a laborious life,
I have continued my devotion
   to the cause of Art.

The writing stopped for a moment and then started again in broken bits.

   For the latter
      I have been
   neither the worst

   nor the best of men

190

but I affirm that
I have never been
more fulfilled
in my life

The writing broke off, next to a series of faded black dots.

"What is it?" Gina asked.

"He stopped writing," Nathan said. "Look at these ink stains. It must be where he set his pen down."

"In the middle of a sentence?" Gina asked, shaking her head in doubt.

Nathan read the first sentence again.

I have been unwell all the day…

The words conjured up a chilling mental image of Raven gasping for breath and looking for the strength to keep writing, all the time knowing that his final breath was just moments away.

"He was too weak to sit up…" Nathan said. "Remember when we looked inside the room, he was slumped forward on the desk?"

Gina nodded quickly and looked away. Then another image flashed in Nathan's mind.

"The candles…"

"Huh?"

"That's why the candles were nothing but globs of wax. They burned themselves out because Raven never got up to extinguish them."

Gina looked back at the letter.

"Look how the writing changes," she said, pointing to the uneven handwriting and the broken sentences. The ink had become lighter, an indication that Raven was fading, struggling to form each letter.

I shall always consider

architecture

the soul

of mankind,

that which holds good

the spirit of

humanity

Once again the writing stopped, only to begin again in a broken pattern of random thoughts. Nathan and Gina cringed as they read it.

It is a great

privilege and

pleasure

to honor

that spirit

Raven's time was running out.

with

tributes

in

kind.

Gina eyes were filled with tears as she turned away. Raven was dying right before their eyes, and she couldn't read another word.

Nathan didn't have a choice.

He had to finish—he had to read it all.

The words were sparse now, an indication that Raven's struggle was near its end. When Nathan finished the letter, he sat motionless for several long moments, reading the last sentence again and again. They were the final thoughts and the last words of Alastair Raven.

Should they endure

the ravages

of time

may they

inspire others

and lead them

to greater

achievements.

"Are you ok, Nathan?" his Dad asked.

Nathan nodded his head. As sad as the letter was, he knew a great deal of good would come from their discovery. "They'll have to rewrite the history books now," he said, staring at the letter.

"That's right," his father replied. "And not only that, think of all the people who will be inspired by this historic building."

"That's what he wanted," Nathan said.

"And you two made it happen," his mother said proudly.

Nathan's mood began to lift.

"What did he mean by 'tributes'?" Ferguson asked.

"This wasn't his only building in town," Nathan answered.

The mayor's face lit up. "What did you say?"

"There are others. We found the blueprints for them in Raven's library."

Chuck paused for a moment and looked up from his notepad. *There are more?*

As they spoke, Gina noticed something unusual about the letter and carefully pried it out of Nathan's hand. She examined it closely for several seconds, holding it up in the air against the bright light of the morning sky.

"Look at this," she exclaimed.

"What is it?" Nathan asked.

"It's an imprint of some kind."

Ferguson leaned closer for a better look. "That's called a watermark. It's not the kind of thing you find on ordinary paper. It's more often found on very fancy or expensive stationery."

"I've seen this name before," Gina said, looking over at Nathan.

"What name?"

She held the paper up towards the sky so he could see the watermark more clearly.

"*That* name," she said, pointing to the middle of the paper.

Buried in the fabric of the paper, just visible behind the ink spots and ragged writing was the outline of a name.

"The Vearn Trust?"

Gina didn't answer—she sat there with a look of complete astonishment.

"What's wrong, dear?" her mother asked.

"The Vearn Trust," she whispered to Nathan. "I saw the exact same name...in that old book."

"You mean, when we were at the Town Hall?" Nathan asked.

"The Town Hall?" Gina's father asked in a loud voice. "Since when do...?"

"Calm down," Gina's mother said, "let her finish."

Gina pointed to the watermark. "This name was on the next page."

"Huh?"

"You remember when the town clerk told us who built the courthouse?"

"Yeah."

"Then I took the book from her and checked the name for myself?"

"I guess..." Nathan said.

"It was when I wrote down Vasari's full name in my notepad?"

"Yeah...OK."

"I saw some numbers. It was how much the town paid to have the courthouse built. But then I looked at the next page. I saw *another* column of numbers."

"What numbers?"

"It was list of monies *received* by the town that year."

"Received?"

"Yes," Gina said, "The Vearn Trust was on that list."

"But that could have just been..."

"No," Gina said, cutting him off, "you don't understand. The amounts were identical."

Nathan looked at the watermark, thinking for a moment, and then looked back at Gina.

"So you think he...?"

"Yes," Gina answered, before he could finish. She knew exactly what he was thinking.

"Well...he didn't need the money," Nathan said, "plus...he was sick...."

"And dying," Gina added.

"Are you saying what I think you're saying?" Ferguson asked.

"The town paid him the money, but he gave it back," Gina said. "He just did it under another..." She stopped mid-sentence.

"What?" Nathan asked.

Gina held the paper up so she could read the watermark again, pointing to each letter in random order.

"It *was* him," she whispered.

"What are you talking about?"

"The name Vearn...it's Raven...just rearranged."

The mayor stood frozen in place, staring at the courthouse in utter disbelief. It was the news story to end all news stories in the entire state. In the entire region. Maybe even the entire country. "You mean to say he built that building for FREE...and nobody knew?"

"It looks that way," Ferguson replied.

The mayor began to pace back and forth, mumbling rapidly in broken sentences. "He'll be a hero...we'll have to erect a statue...this building will be a landmark...people will want to..." He stopped. pacing. "Wait a minute." He turned and looked at Nathan, "You said there were *other* buildings...what other buildings?"

"The library," Gina said.

"The railroad station…" Nathan added.

The mayor didn't wait for them to finish—he spun around and grabbed Chuck Gerard by the arm just as he reached the last page in his notebook. They quickly disappeared down the street, the mayor jabbering excitedly about a full page article for the Sunday edition.

"This is quite a story," Ferguson said, looking at his notes. "Let me see if I've got this right. Famous New York City architect...disappears without a trace...changes his name...relocates and continues to build...apparently for *free*...and all from the confines of a hidden series of rooms beneath the courthouse."

Nathan and Gina nodded their heads in agreement.

"It doesn't make any sense," Ferguson concluded.

"Actually I think it does," Nathan said. "All he wanted to do was see his designs come to life. It was more important to him than anything else."

"He said something about greed," Gina offered. "Do you think everything around him got to be too much?"

"Well, judging from the fact that he dropped out of society completely," Ferguson said, "there was *something* he didn't like."

Nathan's mother added, "To make that drastic a change and not tell anyone? To just walk away?"

"I think it's fair to assume he knew about his illness when he disappeared," the Medical Examiner explained. "That could easily have affected his decision as well."

"He disappeared to spend what time he had left doing what he loved," Nathan replied.

"But how did he build all those other buildings?" Ferguson asked. "For that matter, how did he build *that* one?" he added, pointing to the courthouse.

"At the time this building was constructed," Nathan's father explained, "there was a large influx of immigrants into the area. They were very skilled and very anxious to find work. If Raven was looking for a dedicated work force, there was no shortage of suitable applicants. He could have hired *two* crews if he wanted to—one to work by day and one to work at night."

"If that's the case," Ferguson suggested, "I imagine he kept a record of wages he paid out."

"That would make sense," Nathan's father replied. "Maybe you'll find them when you search his desk."

Detective Ferguson shook his head in amazement. "This just gets better by the minute."

Nathan stood up and handed Detective Ferguson the letter.

By the time they were done searching the hidden rooms in the courthouse, the wage records would be one of hundreds of documents found. In the weeks that followed, as those documents were carefully examined, they would reveal how Raven spent his remaining time and riches building elaborate constructions, working tirelessly despite a life-threatening illness and giving every penny he received back to the town through a series of anonymous donations.

"I still don't get it," Ferguson said, as he slipped the letter into a plastic evidence bag. "Why all the secrecy?"

"Simple," Nathan replied. "He wanted the focus to be on the buildings and the style...not who built them."

Gina was staring at the magnificent front entrance of the courthouse, remembering the feeling of awe she had when she first stood before it earlier in the week. "It was beauty for beauty's sake," she said.

"What now?" Nathan asked the detective.

Ferguson signaled to Officer Briggs, who was leaning on the hood of his police cruiser parked several feet away. Then he turned to Nathan and Gina. "I need you both to go with Officer Briggs." The look on his face was very serious.

Nathan gulped. "Wait...are we...in trouble?"

What about the newspaper?

Our photos?

He looked over at Gina, whose face was as pale as his.

"Because we were just..."

"Officer Briggs?" Ferguson said, ignoring Nathan.

"Come on," Briggs said, motioning both kids towards the cruiser.

Nathan and Gina stood up, their bodies trembling as they walked slowly away from the group. Their parents stood by and watched silently as they climbed into the back of the cruiser and Briggs closed the door.

Then he took them away.

Chapter Thirteen

HB

Nathan slumped back in the seat as the police cruiser pulled away from the courthouse.

Was this really happening?

We save this historic building from being destroyed...

People turned and watched them as they drove by.

And this is the thanks we get?

What about that thing the mayor said, about the town owing them a debt of gratitude?

A huge debt of gratitude, to be exact.

This sure was a funny way to show it.

After they passed through the roadblock at the end of the street, Briggs chirped the siren several times to clear the mob that had gathered in the road. It was a piercing bird-like shriek that jolted Nathan out of his stupor, and for the first time since getting in the vehicle he took stock of the cramped surroundings.

Staring him in the face was a thick wire mesh, separating the back seat from the front. He looked to his right—there was no door handle. The window glass was scuffed and dirty, protected by a framework of narrow steel bars. And what was that stench? It smelled like lemon dish soap and rotten cabbage.

He tried to ignore it as he turned and stared out the window, watching the storefronts on Main Street float past in slow motion. What was going to happen to them? Were they going to jail? Would it be in the newspapers? What would their parents say? Officer Briggs hadn't uttered a word since they left the courthouse. He was just driving along, like it was any other day, lightly tapping his fingers on the steering wheel and watching the traffic. At any moment Nathan expected him to start whistling a merry tune.

Gina sat motionless on the seat with her arms crossed and her head drooped forward, staring at the floor with an angry scowl. This was the *exact thing* she wanted to avoid, for both of them, when she raced down to the courthouse to "save" Nathan. But she failed. And now, on top of everything else they'd been through, they were being carted away in the back of a police cruiser like common criminals.

This is SO embarrassing.

She slid down farther in the seat hoping no one would recognize her through the side window.

Chuck Gerard was frantically typing at his computer when he heard a voice.

"I didn't see you come back in."

It was Frank, standing a few feet away. He was eyeing Gerard's notes, a jumble of handwriting with numerous underlined words and circled names. Without looking up, Gerard flipped to the next page and kept typing. "I had to get back here as fast as I could. This is amazing."

Frank stepped forward and peered over Gerard's shoulder. The senior reporter had called in earlier from the courthouse, telling Frank to save the front page for a "blockbuster" story. When he read the headline of Gerard's story, his jaw fell open in shock.

ARCHITECT'S SECRET REVEALED!
Courthouse demolition halted following startling
discovery of hidden rooms, human remains

Gerard was busy transposing his notes and never saw his boss pull up a chair and sit down next to him, devouring every word on the computer monitor. This was more than just a front page story—it would very quickly go national and get picked up by every news organization in the country.

And we're going to break the story, he thought with a smile.

Briggs drove casually through town and called in his location on the radio when they approached the police station. It was a modern two-story building set back from the road by a spacious and well-kept lawn. The parking lot on the side of the building, usually lined with police cruisers, was completely empty. There was no need to ask where they were.

He signaled with the blinker and touched the brakes before turning into the entrance. That's when the reality of the situation hit Nathan like a punch in the gut.

They're going to fingerprint us.

His body began to tremble.

We're going to be locked up in a cell.

He started to feel nauseous.

We'll be grounded for life.

Alfred M. Struthers

He buried his face in his hands, wishing it was all just a bad dream, one that he would wake from at any moment.

Briggs pulled up to the side door and stopped a few feet away—close enough so neither of the kids could make a run for it. The radio chatter continued nonstop and he turned down the volume just before he opened the door and climbed out. Then he turned around and ducked his head back inside the car.

"Be right back," he said. "I need to pick something up at the front desk."

Nathan and Gina both looked up.

"Excuse me?" Gina said.

Without answering, Briggs closed the door and went inside the station.

They sat speechless for several long seconds. The only sound in the car was the police radio, but with the volume turned down, the voices were muffled and distant. It sounded like someone watching a movie downstairs in the living room, late at night. Gina turned to Nathan, her eyebrows knit with confusion. "Be right back?"

Nathan had a puzzled look on his face, like he had just detected a foul odor. "Pick something up?"

"What in the world is...?" Gina started to ask.

Before she could finish, the door opened and Briggs climbed back into the car. He set a black plastic camera case on the passenger seat and then looked at both kids in the rear view mirror—just like their school bus driver. "OK," he said, "now we can go."

Nathan looked at Gina, baffled, and then at Officer Briggs. "Uh...excuse me..." he stammered, "...but...where exactly are we going?"

204

Briggs twisted around in his seat and stared at Nathan for a moment, then Gina, then back at Nathan again.

What is this, a joke?

He shrugged his shoulders. "Home, of course."

They both perked up at once, their eyes bright with surprise. And relief.

"You mean...we're not...?" Gina began to say.

"Not what?" Briggs asked.

"Arrested?" Nathan said.

"Wait," Briggs said, "you thought...?" He started to laugh out loud, then turned around and started the car. "No," he said as he pulled away from the side door and circled around behind the building, "you are definitely *not* being arrested."

"But we were trespassing," Nathan said.

Gina flicked him hard on the arm. *Don't REMIND him!*

Nathan flinched and twisted away, grabbing his arm that now stung with pain.

"I thought Ferguson explained it to you before we left," Briggs said. "He and the mayor agreed not to file any charges."

"That was very nice of them," Gina replied. She glared at Nathan.

"Well...I'd say the discovery you made had a lot to do with that," he said , as he stopped at the end of the driveway. The steady line of Saturday traffic crept nervously past the police cruiser and it was almost a full minute before Briggs could pull out.

"So why did Ferguson make us go with you?" Nathan asked.

"Why?" he asked, like it was a silly question. "Did you see the crowd? News like this travels very fast. Chuck Gerard

205

was only one reporter, but I bet there are at least a *dozen* of them down there now. Maybe even more."

"I don't understand," Nathan said.

"Ferguson knew if we didn't sneak you out of there right away, it would've been a very long day for the two of you...*and* your parents. And I don't think they need any more excitement. Not today."

"Good thinking," Nathan mumbled. He looked over at Gina, who nodded in agreement. This ordeal wasn't over for either of them. Not by a long shot. There would be interviews, follow up stories, and more discoveries in the Raven's secret chamber.

Several minutes later they reached Nathan's house. Briggs pulled the cruiser up to the curb and called in his location on the police radio. Just as he was finishing, Nathan's parents pulled into the driveway. Gina's parents were with them.

When Briggs saw them, he quickly got out of the cruiser and opened the back door.

"Thank you," Gina said as she climbed out.

"Yeah, thanks," Nathan quipped. He stood next to the cruiser and puffed out his chest. "I feel like a rock star."

"In your dreams," Gina said, rolling her eyes. If she was closer she would've flicked him again.

Their parents came over and thanked Officer Briggs for his help. They had been briefed at the scene by Detective Ferguson, so Briggs got back in the cruiser and disappeared down the street.

For several seconds there was an awkward moment of silence. Then Nathan's father said, "So...Nathan...you never did tell us what made you go down to the courthouse in the first place."

Nathan's rock star smile dissolved into an expression of dread. Gina looked down at the sidewalk, grinding the toe of her sneaker into the tar like she was squashing a bug.

"You know, I was wondering that, too," Nathan's mother said, eyeing him suspiciously. "You said you were studying that architect. What was his name? Alastair Raven?"

Nathan looked up to see everyone staring at him, waiting for an answer.

"Well...actually..." he began and then paused.

"It *wasn't* Raven," Gina blurted out. She glanced at Nathan, both eyebrows raised. *Agree with me...*

"Uh...yeah..." he stammered, staring at Gina while he spoke, "it wasn't him." His eyes were wide with anticipation. *Huh?*

Gina held his gaze and spoke slowly, nodding her head with every word.

"We - were - studying - Gothic - architecture...?"

Nathan thought for a moment. Then he got it.

"That's right," he exclaimed, his eyes still locked on hers. "And we...um...*noticed* some examples on the courthouse building." *How's that?*

Gina nodded, rolling her eyes at the same time. *Took you long enough.*

"And that's what made you go to the town clerk..." Gina's mother said, putting the pieces together.

"Exactly," Gina said, very matter-of-factly.

"Oh...that's right," Nathan's father said, "that's where you got the name of the builder...did the word thing...found out it was really the other guy...I get it now."

Nathan let out a heavy breath.

"That was pretty impressive," his mother said.

"Well...we'll have a long talk about that later," Gina's father huffed.

"Enough already," her mother added quickly. She looked at Nathan's mother and shrugged her shoulders in frustration.

Nathan's mother quickly changed the subject. "Who's ready for some lunch?"

That brought an immediate response from the others and they walked across the lawn and disappeared into Nathan's house.

Nathan and Gina stayed outside in the driveway and unloaded their bikes from the back of the car. When they were done, Gina turned to Nathan and said, "I owe you an apology."

"An apology? What for?"

"For the way I acted this week. For some reason...I don't know...I just didn't want to believe in that book. When I saw it in your basement, it scared me."

"Yeah, well, it scared me too, but I..."

"Then you stopped TALKING to me...and you got me in TROUBLE!" She reached over and punched him in the arm.

"Yeah, sorry about that," he said, kicking at the tar. Then he looked up at her and said, "But I couldn't stop. Not after you figured out Raven's name from that town report. That's when I knew that I had to keep going. There was something in the courthouse that I had to find."

"Well, I have to admit, it turned out to be pretty exciting," she said. "To tell you the truth, I'm kind of sorry it's over."

"Yeah, me too," Nathan said.

"Oh, I almost forgot," she said, reaching behind her back. "I meant to give you something."

"What is it?"

"I'm not sure." She fumbled with something in her back pocket, and when she brought her arm forward again she was holding a narrow slip of paper. It was an inch wide and roughly five inches long, made from a heavy paper stock that was wrinkled and worn with age. "I found it in the passageway," she said, handing it to him.

Nathan took the slip of paper and examined it closely. There was some printing on it, but it had faded over time and it was impossible to decipher. Then he flipped it over. His eyes went wide and his jaw fell open in disbelief.

"Are you ok?" Gina asked.

"Wh-where did you say…you f-found this?"

"It was in the passageway, on the floor by the stone door. I found it when we were looking for a way out. I completely forgot about it until just now."

Nathan staggered over to the grass and collapsed on the lawn.

"What's wrong?" Gina asked, hurrying over to his side.

He reached out with a trembling hand and gave her the paper so she could see it for herself. "See those letters?"

Gina looked closely and saw two letters embossed on one end of the paper. They were set vertically, in a thick serif font and she had to turn the paper to read them.

"…H…B…?"

She looked at Nathan and shrugged. *Two letters…big deal.*

Nathan stared at her with a dazed look on his face, as a faded memory came to life in his mind. It flickered through his memory like an old black and white film reel.

Click-click-click.

It was long ago. Longer than he could remember, or so it seemed. One of his earliest memories. He was four years old. Or was he five? He was riding with his grandfather in the truck. They were coming back from a trip to some remote village in Western Massachusetts that had taken the better part of the day. His recollection was vague; but they were in a food store. No, it was a bookstore. His grandfather was talking to the man behind the counter. Then they were loading boxes into the back of the truck. Open boxes. Heavy. Too heavy for him to lift. Each one was filled with old books.

They drove back home, stopping in town on the way. It was a narrow street. Small shops lined both sides. It was just a quick stop. "This won't take a minute," his grandfather told him. Nathan stayed in the truck and watched as his grandfather unlocked the heavy glass-paneled door and lugged the boxes inside.

As he watched and waited, he looked up and saw it—the sign hanging over the door. It was the letters that caught his eye. He had no idea what they meant but they held his attention until his grandfather returned.

Two letters.

Matching type face.

Gold leaf.

Glittering in the afternoon sun that spilled over a nearby rooftop like a long strip of cotton gauze.

"HB," he said to Gina in a weak voice, his face the color of milk. "Hammond Books."

"What?"

"My grandfather's bookstore."

Gina didn't say a word.

"My grandfather was Henry Hammond."

Gina's eyes lit up and she handed him the paper, as if it were a royal document.

210

"This is a bookmark from his store." He stared at the letters, remembering that late afternoon and the way the letters sparkled in the sunlight.

Gina looked at the bookmark. Then back at Nathan. "That means he…" she began.

"Exactly," Nathan said, "he found the passageway."

They both sat there without speaking for several seconds.

"What if it was just someone who had been to his store?" Gina suggested.

"No," Nathan said with conviction. There was more to it, and it made complete sense now. "You found this near the entrance to the passageway?"

"Yeah, it was wedged underneath the stone door. I was pulling it out when the door began to open."

Nathan stared at her with that same look of certainty she'd seen before.

"My grandfather was looking for Raven. He found the passageway and marked the exit with *this*," he said, holding up the bookmark. "That way he'd know how to get…" He stopped short as the rest of it came to him.

Only one bookmark…not two…

Gina sat there waiting for him to finish, but he was staring into the street, his face void of expression.

"What is it?"

"He never found it…" Nathan whispered, turning to look at her. His eyes were fixed with a look of certainty, one that sent chills up and down both of her arms.

"Huh?"

"My grandfather…he never found it."

"Found what?"

"The second door."

"What second door?"

"The one with the gargoyle," Nathan said. "He never made it into the hidden rooms."

Gina thought about that for a moment, but Nathan quickly let it go as his mind worked through something even more startling. It was huge—the ninth inning variety.

His bookshop...

It was a game changer.

His bookcase...

The grand slam over the fence.

His book...

Game over.

He turned to Gina—shell-shocked. "I was wrong," he said slowly, the realization pulsing through his mind. "It wasn't Raven."

"Huh?"

His face felt cold, like someone had wrapped a wet dishcloth around it.

"Raven wasn't the one who wanted me to find the secret chamber."

"Not Raven? What are you talking about?"

"It was my grandfather," he said, looking up at her, "from the very start."

"What?...no way," she scoffed, rolling her eyes.

But Nathan just nodded his head slowly—the look on his face was unwavering.

"The bookcase in the attic...my mom said it was from his bookstore."

"You never told me that," Gina said. A nervous jolt shot through her body.

"The book was lying there on the floor...where he knew I'd see it."

212

Gina crossed her arms and bit her knuckle as a cold shiver raced up her spine.

"I tried to put it back on the shelf, but he wouldn't let me. He kept pushing…giving me clue after clue."

He spoke for nearly five minutes straight, telling her every detail he'd been afraid to tell her before—the things he was sure would drive her away—but she sat in stunned silence, hanging on every word. When he was done, he paused a moment to let it all sink in. His chance meeting with the book on the third floor had been anything but a coincidence.

"He wanted me to finish it, Gina…"

"Finish…?"

"He wanted me to finish what he started. He wanted me to find Raven's secret."

Gina's gaze fell away, and she stared blankly at the grass near her feet. Nathan was staring at the ground as well, reliving the entire episode, all the while putting a new face to it—the weathered image of a man he hardly knew.

It took several minutes but Gina finally looked up at Nathan. He was still staring at the ground, but there was a completely different look on his face. The dazed expression was gone, as if every memory he'd been reliving had drained out of his mind, like water from a leaky pail. In its place was the look of unflinching certainty.

"I'll prove it," he said, climbing to his feet. Before Gina could get up, he turned and walked towards the house.

"WAIT," she yelled, scrambling to get up.

Together they walked into the house and went straight upstairs. When they reached his bedroom Nathan walked over to the bedside table and picked up the book. He never saw the pillowcase lying near the desk. Gina would tell him about that later. Maybe.

They rushed down the hall until they came to the attic stairs. Nathan went first, ignoring the painful moans of each stair tread. This time, when he reached the attic door, it wasn't like his previous visits—he didn't feel a sense of dread as he stepped into the darkness and tasted the stale air. The attic was nothing compared to the dark passageway in the basement of the courthouse.

He ignored the spider webs and mountains of dust-covered boxes and went directly over to bookcase.

"Now I know," he whispered as he stood before it, eyeing it from top to bottom. It was no longer just some outdated relic hidden in the shadows on the third floor.

"It was you…"

And it wasn't just the *book* that was haunted.

"You were the one guiding me…"

It was the bookcase.

"Grampa."

He opened the book and placed the bookmark next to the photo of Alastair Raven. For several seconds he stood and stared at the faded picture of the architectural master and the page that started the whole adventure. One thing was certain, this was one book he'd never forget.

Mystery solved.

He closed the book and lifted it towards the bookcase. Something pushed back.

"Hey!"

He tried again, but an invisible force was repelling the book and keeping his arm from moving forward.

"What's the matter?" Gina asked.

"I don't know," he replied, looking into the open slot on the shelf. It wasn't like before, when he put the book on the shelf and it refused to stay there. This was altogether different.

"Just put it back," she said.

"I'm trying to, but something's blocking it."

"Blocking it?" She rolled her eyes. "Nonsense. Here, let me try."

"Suit yourself," he said, handing her the book.

She stepped up to the bookcase. "You know...sometimes," she said, shaking her head as she turned the book upright to slide it into the opening, "I wonder how you even..."

The book bucked in her hand.

"See?" Nathan asked.

Her heart began to beat faster. She took a deep breath and tried again, but this time the book lurched back at her with enough force to drive her hand back into her body. She shrieked and let go of it as a faint tingling sensation rippled up her forearm, all the way to her elbow.

But that wasn't the strangest part.

They both stood frozen in place, their jaws dropped open in astonishment.

"Nathan?" she said in a thin high-pitched voice. "Why is it doing that?"

The book was hovering in front of the bookcase, hanging in midair as if suspended by invisible wires.

"Uh..." he said in a shaky voice, trying to think of what to say next.

Gina backed away without taking her eyes from the book and nearly fell over when she bumped against a short stack of plastic tubs. She let out a gasp when the book began to move sideways through the air, floating slowly but steadily towards Nathan.

When it was close enough to touch, he reached out and carefully took hold of it. He stared at it momentarily and then looked up at the bookcase as the realization slowly dawned on him.

"He doesn't want it back."

"What do you mean?"

His eyes moved from book to book along the top shelf as something his mother said echoed in his mind.

"Special editions," he whispered.

"What did you say?"

"I asked why my grandfather kept these books." As he spoke he scanned the rows of old books, shelf by shelf. "My mother said they were special editions."

Gina bit the edge of her lip.

He ran his fingertips along the edge of the first shelf, feeling the satin finish of the smooth dark grain. If the rest of the books were anything like *Compton's Journal*, concealing long forgotten mysteries...

Not mysteries, he thought to himself. *Secrets*.

A case of secrets.

Just like Raven kept...hidden away all these years...in his secret library.

In that moment the full meaning was clear.

"This doesn't belong here now," he said, shifting his gaze towards Gina.

"Doesn't *belong*?"

"We solved the mystery. This book doesn't belong here with the others."

"OK...I have *no* idea what you're talking about."

"No matter," he said, looking back down at the book in his hands. He was picturing the short wooden bookcase in his bedroom where he kept his baseball trophies. "I have the perfect spot for it."

He looked up at the bookcase, overcome with a curious mixture of awe and disbelief. It wasn't just from the book, or the amazing events at the courthouse; it was the ancient relic that stood before him—an ordinary-looking bookcase, right here in his own house, filled with books that were anything but ordinary. Quite the opposite.

Then it hit him.

Something his mother said in the basement. It was about the bookcase, and his heart beat faster as her words churned madly in his mind.

"He was very fond of it."

But there was something more.

"Probably because it belonged to his father."

And the mystery of the bookcase became even bigger.

"Your great grandfather."

"What's wrong?" Gina asked.

He didn't answer. He continued to stare at the bookcase, his curiosity peaked, as a question formed in his mind.

Where did it come from?

Then another.

Who started collecting these books?

And another.

Was it my great grandfather?

And another still.

Or was it someone before him?

"HEY," Gina said. She poked his shoulder with two fingers. Hard. "Are you going to stand there all day with your mouth open?"

Her words broke his train of thought, sending the whirlwind of questions deep into a remote corner of his mind. For the time being. Someday, in the not too distant future, he'd find the answers to these and many other questions.

His stomach growled.

"Are you hungry?" he asked.

"Starving."

"Come on, let's go eat lunch."

They started to leave when Gina said, "Oh look."

"What?" Nathan said, stopping to turn around.

"No wait, don't move, I'll get it."

He let out a heavy sigh as she grabbed the back of his head with one hand and pushed it forward. The barber did it all the time. It was very annoying. With her other hand she began tugging at his hair. The barber did that all the time, too.

It was just as bad.

"HEY," he said, trying to squirm away. But she had a hold of his head and wouldn't let go.

"Just hold still. Will you?"

Moments later she turned his head around with a turn of her wrist and dangled a fat brown spider just inches from his face. It was the size of a quarter and its legs were moving wildly, trying to get free. He jumped back and began slapping at the long strands of hair on both sides of his head, in case there were others hiding in there that she didn't see.

"That does it," he said, "I'm getting a haircut."

Gina didn't respond—she was too busy playing with the spider, letting it run over her wrist and then snatching it up before it could scurry up her arm.

When Nathan was convinced that his scraggly hair was free of any unwanted spiders, he made his way towards the door. He was careful to scan back and forth and overhead as

218

he walked, so the spiders stayed behind...where they belonged.

They were almost to the door when a loud thud broke the stillness of the dusty room and they both spun around to see a book lying on the floor.

It had fallen out of the bookcase.

Second shelf.

Epilogue

The storm continued to rage outside the shop windows when Samuel Hammond finished sorting the wagonload of books. He shelved the smaller pile, a total of four books, on the old bookcase in the corner where only he would have access to them.

The remaining books would have to wait, due to the vast number, until the next day. He would clean the cover of each one with a soft cloth and then price them, making a discrete notation inside the front flap with his red cedar pencil.

He wandered through the shop and peered out at the restless night, through one of the small rain-soaked panes in the front window. A spiteful blast of wind was whipping the shop's heavy oaken sign back and forth like a thin silk ribbon. The muted squeak of its hinges were barely audible over the howling gale. He checked the clock on the near wall—it was still early. Best to wait out the storm for just a while longer before heading home.

He returned to the back room and settled into the heavy wooden chair behind his desk, a stately roll top fashioned from rich black walnut. From one of the side drawers he extracted a thin, leather-bound book, no more than an inch thick. It was a fairly recent acquisition, barely six months in his possession. He had unearthed it from the bottom of a crate packed with books, purchased at an auction in Wiscasset, Maine.

On the cover was a single name. It was elegantly written in black ink that was scratched and faded from years of handling.

Henrietta

The shop windows rattled nervously as he opened the fragile cover and removed a folded letter. It came to him earlier in the week from a local historian in Bath, Maine, to whom he had sent an inquiry, shortly after examining the book.

The letter chronicled the tragic account of a schooner that set sail from Yarmouth, Nova Scotia, in the winter of 1845, under the command of Captain William Carver, its captain and owner. During the voyage, a vicious nor'easter forced Carver's ship off course and it ran aground on Ragged Island, just south of Matinicus Isle on outer Penobscot Bay.

The lifeless bodies of the captain and crew were found the following spring, holed up in a small cave near Bull Cove. Just offshore, battered but not defeated, the ship sat upright at a curious angle, caught in the grip of the jagged rocks that lurked below the waves.

Because no surviving family members could be found, a Maine court awarded the ship and all of its contents, by salvage rights, to the fisherman who discovered it. He promptly repaired the vessel and sailed south to warmer climates, where he started a new life far away from the frigid Maine winters.

And that's where the story ended.

Despite an exhaustive search, the historian could find no information on the current whereabouts, let alone the existence, of the ship. He concluded that the new owner, fearing the boat was cursed, broke with nautical tradition and renamed it.

The proud schooner, *Henrietta,* had sailed her final voyage.

Several years later, a local geologist exploring the caves on Ragged Island would discover the ship's log, tucked in a narrow crevice, just inches away from where William Carver took his final breath. With little interest in ship lore, the book quickly found a home in the geologist's attic, buried in a box of outdated textbooks.

Samuel folded the letter and set it aside. The battered leather cover of the captain's log felt ominous to his touch. Perhaps *Henrietta* was cursed after all. In his own words, Carver explained how he named the ship after his only daughter, who later died of smallpox; recounted the brutality of the winter storm that pounded the ship like an angry fist; the struggle of the crew to survive in the blistering cold with a rapidly diminishing food supply.

But something else sparked Samuel's curiosity.

Buried among the long list of latitudes and longitudes, wind conditions, distances and unusual sightings, he found several cryptic entries that referred to part of *Henrietta's* cargo. The handwriting was erratic, but Carver made mention, in serious tone, of a container "overladen with property of substantial volume, which required risk to obtain."

In earlier entries, Carver mentioned a small island off the south coast of Nova Scotia, visited often by a group he described as "adversaries at sea." The captain's ragged handwriting made it nearly impossible to decipher, but Samuel was convinced he was referring to Star Island, long rumored to be a haven for pirates' buried treasure.

And in the most intriguing entry of all, Carver described a hidden compartment aboard the ship, one of "good appearance, known to none but myself." He went on to claim, in a tone that was boastful and proud, that "no man shall discover its location, but by my direction."

The wall clock chimed the top of the hour, breaking Samuel's concentration. He had been reading for well over an hour. It was time to go home. He slipped the letter into the ship's log and placed it back in the side drawer. But as he extinguished the lanterns on his desk, his thoughts continued to churn.

What new name had the owner given the schooner? Was she making headway, her sails cupped in the wind, or was she wasting away in a cradle, her keel cracking in the sun, in some boatyard halfway around the world?

Of one thing he was certain. To this day she carried in her belly a pirate's fortune, salvaged from a small atoll off the western shores of Big Tancook Island. And no one knew.

Yet.

As he emerged from the back room, the only sound to be heard was the gentle ticking of the wall clock. Outside, the shop's sign held a silent vigil, the letters "HB" shining in the clear moonlight like polished copper.

He stopped at one of the bookshelves that lined the outer wall of the shop and selected a storybook for his young son, Nathaniel. It was an immaculate first edition signed by the author, L. Frank Baum. Little did he know, as he wrapped it in paper and secured it with string, that the storybook would become one of Nathaniel's most prized possessions.

In time he would pass it on to another—one whose love of books was equal to his own.

His son...Henry Hammond.

Tesserae

♦The Gothic Revival came to America from England around 1830 and featured elements of medieval period architecture.

♦Giorgio Vasari was a painter, writer, historian and architect who lived in Italy during the 16th century.

♦In the United States, up until about 1870, few architects had college educations. They were carpenters, tradesmen, or those educated in design through apprenticeship, reading, extensive travel, or other means. Only toward the end of the 19th century did architects begin to receive professional educations.

♦Alastair Raven and Franklin Jarratt are fictional characters.

♦Richard Morris Hunt (1827-1895) was born in Brattleboro, Vermont, and became one of New York's most prominent architects. Of his numerous designs, two of the most notable include the 5th Avenue facade of the Metropolitan Museum of Art and the pedestal of the Statue of Liberty. In 1857, he helped establish the American Institute of Architects (AIA).

♦Chimera is pronounced "Kih-MEAR-ah."

♦Gargoyles originated somewhere between the 11th and 13th centuries. They served two purposes: to scare off evil and to divert rainwater.

♦The Pacific Crest Trail, Appalachian Trail, and Continental Divide Trail are the three U.S. long distance hiking trails informally referred to as the Triple Crown of Hiking.

♦Ragged Island, in Knox County, Maine, was incorporated as the plantation of Criehaven in 1896, by Robert Crie (1825-1901), who moved there in 1849 with his wife, Harriet Hall. In 1925, Criehaven reverted to an unorganized territory and to this day is home to seasonal fishermen and vacationers.

♦According to sailors' legend, changing the name on a boat will anger the God of the Sea and curse the boat with bad luck.

♦By the end of the 19th century, the preferred timber used for making pencils was Red Cedar. It was popular for its aromatic quality and because it wouldn't splinter when sharpened.

♦Captain William Carver is a fictional character, inspired by the legacy of Searsport, Maine. In the 19th and 20th centuries, this small coastal community was home to over 500 merchant captains.

Acknowledgements

My heartfelt thanks go out to the following people, whose help, guidance and support made this book possible:

Kim Dalley, my first reader. For her deep knowledge and unshakable love of literature, we are all very lucky indeed.

My amazing editor, Deb Scott, and the whole team at ACB, who brought *The Case of Secrets* out of hiding at long last.

Lou Waryncia (Cobblestone Press), for his belief, patience and encouragement.

Jim Grant (Staff Development for Educators), for his wisdom and unwavering dedication, and who told me the first thing to remember.

Cheryl Lang, "think partner" extraordinaire, for sharing her ideas, professional expertise and tales from the front line.

The dedicated staff at The Toadstool Bookstore.

Gyakyi Bonsu-Anane, for his time and wizardry with the chapter page illustrations, and for many years of sharing his creativity, which is galactic in scope.

Jackie Craven for her architectural wisdom.

Alison Meltzer, for the right book, a comfortable chair, and all the time I needed to find the perfect word.

Brian Hackert (Research Librarian), for his help with period-specific dialogue, his relentless pursuit of knowledge, and his uncanny ability to find the needle in the haystack.

Craig Fraley, for guiding me through medical response procedures.

Sean O'Malley (Handy Boat, Falmouth , ME) for sharing his vast knowledge of boats and the sea.

Teachers and librarians worldwide—superheroes that live among us!

Young readers the world over, without whom I'd be outside mowing the lawn right now.

And to Karen, my incredible wife, co-pilot and trusted advisor on this amazing journey.

Illustration Credits

The graduated chapter page illustrations form a quatrefoil, which is a common element in Gothic architecture. This version was inspired by a small window in the south wall of the chancel, in the Church of St. Mary the Virgin, Tatsfield, Surrey, England.

The church was constructed in the 12th century and sits on the crest of the North Downs, a ridge of hills in the southeastern region of England.

The idea of using graduated images on the chapter pages was suggested by Karen Struthers and Cheryl Lang. The images were constructed by the author and processed by the expert hand of Gyakyi Bonsu-Anane.

About the Author

Alfred M. Struthers lives in Peterborough, New Hampshire, with his wife and their incorrigible dog, Manny. He loves crafting books that inspire, entertain and make a difference in the lives of young readers. In addition to writing, Mr. Struthers is a singer/songwriter, furniture maker, and avid collector of fossils from the stream beds around Cooperstown, New York. *The Case of Secrets* is his first published novel.

To find out what else he's been up to, please visit:

www.alfredstruthers.com.